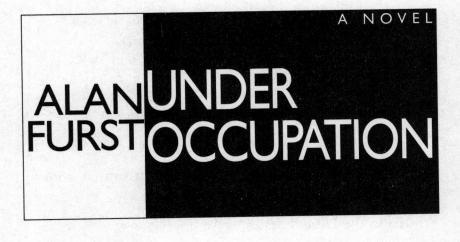

A NOVEL

ALAN FURST

UNDER OCCUPATION

RANDOM HOUSE
LARGE PRINT

Copyright © 2019 by Alan Furst
Maps copyright © 2019 by David Lindroth Inc.

All rights reserved.
Published in the United States of America by Random House Large Print in association with Random House, an imprint and division of Penguin Random House LLC, New York.

Cover design: Carlos Beltrán
Cover photographs: The Image Works (front), Plainpicture/donkeysoho/YBig (back)

The Library of Congress has established a Cataloging-in-Publication record for this title.

ISBN: 978-1-9848-8695-8

www.penguinrandomhouse.com/large-print-format-books

FIRST LARGE PRINT EDITION
Printed in the United States of America

10 9 8 7 6 5 4 3 2 1

This Large Print edition published in accord with the standards of the N.A.V.H.

For Catherine

In 1942, in Nazi-occupied France, the German Occupation Authority rounded up émigré Poles—electricians, welders, machinists—and forced them to work as slave laborers at the naval yards in Kiel, where U-boats were built. The Poles fought back, stealing technical information and smuggling it to Paris, where it was sent on to the British Secret Intelligence Service in London.

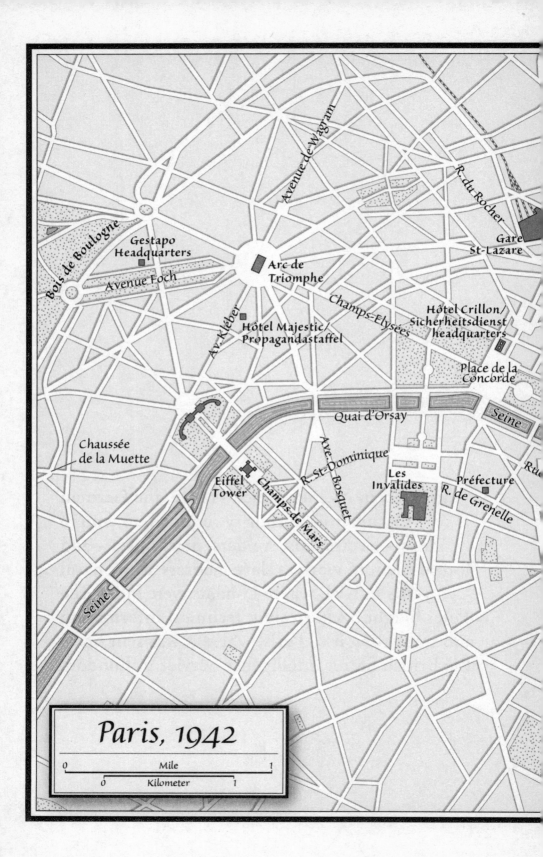

Paris, 1942

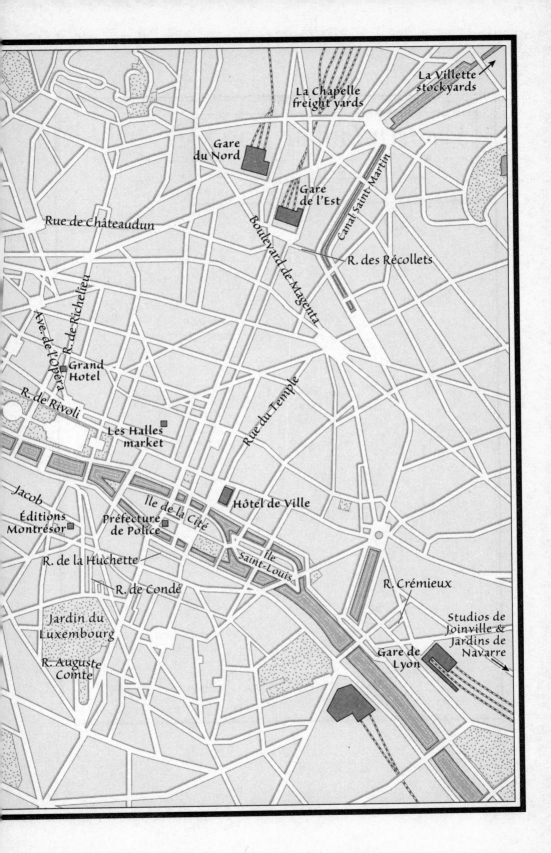

La Villette stockyards

La Chapelle freight yards

Gare du Nord

Gare de l'Est

Canal Saint-Martin

Rue de Châteaudun

Boulevard de Magenta

R. des Récollets

R. de Richelieu

Ave. de l'Opéra

Grand Hôtel

R. de Rivoli

Rue du Temple

Les Halles market

Jacob

Éditions Montrésor

Île de la Cité

Hôtel de Ville

Préfecture de Police

R. de la Huchette

Île Saint-Louis

R. Crémieux

R. de Condé

Jardin du Luxembourg

Studios de Joinville & Jardins de Navarre

Gare de Lyon

R. Auguste Comte

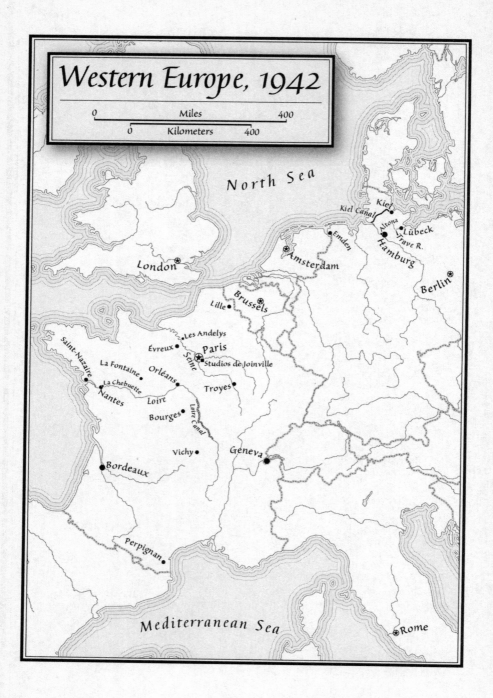

Western Europe, 1942

0   Miles   400

0   Kilometers   400

North Sea

Kiel

Kiel Canal

Altona

Lübeck

Emden

Trave R.

Hamburg

Amsterdam

Berlin

London

Brussels

Lille

Les Andelys

Évreux

Paris

Seine

Studios de Joinville

La Fontaine

Orléans

Troyes

Saint-Nazaire

La Chebuette

Nantes

Loire

Bourges

Loire Canal

Vichy

Geneva

Bordeaux

Perpignan

Mediterranean Sea

Rome

MIDNIGHT IN TRIESTE

At dusk, the freighter tied up at the wharf, the amber streetlamps of the town hazy and dim beyond the port. They stood together at the railing, amid a silence broken only by a distant foghorn and the wash of waves against the pier. She moved closer to him and said, "I never thought we would come back here." In response, he took her hand. Then a ship's officer unhooked the chain at the top of the gangway. It was time to go ashore.

—Paul Ricard, *Midnight in Trieste*

Occupied Paris, 1942.

IN EARLY OCTOBER, THE FIRST OF THE AUTUMN storms began in the late afternoon, with rumbles of thunder up in Normandy somewhere, then, by nightfall, the rain reached Paris, where it beat against the windows of the gray city and streamed down the channels at the edges of the cobblestone streets. The writer Paul Ricard walked bent over in the downpour, headed up a narrow street of ancient buildings in the Sixth Arrondissement: the Rive Gauche, the Latin Quarter.

Ricard squinted into the darkness, some of the

streetlamps had been shattered, others painted blue for the blackout ordered by the German Occupation Authority, and the coal smoke that drifted through the rain made it even harder to see anything. Turning a corner he found himself on the Rue de l'Odéon, once home to Shakespeare and Company, Sylvia Beach's English-language bookstore. But the store had closed a year earlier and now Ricard, a writer of detective and spy fiction, had to get his newly published novels of intrigue at a recently opened store called The Bookshop, on the nearby Rue de Condé. Ricard, rain dripping from the rim of his fedora hat, took a narrow alley to the street—he could reach out and touch the buildings on either side. He was headed for The Bookshop to see a friend who had, voice excited, telephoned and asked that he come see her at the shop.

When Ricard entered the bookstore, his friend, an émigré Pole called Kasia, was manning the cashier's desk near the door. In her twenties, Kasia looked like a Parisian street kid: she had dark eyes and dark hair cut short—a boy's haircut—atop a firm, well-curved body. She wore a worker's tweed cap, a navy pea jacket—likely bought at a used-clothing barrow—mole-colored trousers, and ankle-high, lace-up boots. Ricard nodded to her and waited while she served a customer, a German officer, tall and stern. **"Delta of Venus,"** she said to the officer, "in fact all the Anaïs Nin erotica, is written for a private collector, so it's not available."

"Oh, is that so." The officer was clearly disappointed.

"But we carry a book, a kind of diary, that's similar. Would you care to have a look at it?"

"Why yes"—the German visibly brightened—"I would love to see it."

Kasia looked at Ricard as she left the desk and raised her eyes to heaven: **yet one more German trying to buy dirty books.** She left the desk, walked over to the shelves, and returned with a slim volume. On the soft cover, an artful line drawing of a nude couple in a complicated embrace. "Here it is," she said. "**The Diary of Lady X**, it is erotica for every taste, and lavishly illustrated."

"Thank you," said the German, in school French. "This will do very nicely." Ricard could think of nothing but the well-known quote from the rogue publisher Maurice Girodias, who described such works as "books that one reads with one hand." The German paid Kasia and left the store with his new book wrapped in a sheet of newspaper.

"That's the tenth copy we've sold this week," Kasia said to Ricard. "The Boche come to Paris with lists—the best restaurants, the fanciest brothels, and where to buy books that get them ready for the brothels. Where they especially like exhibitions."

"They've conquered Europe, so they can do whatever they like. They think."

Kasia shrugged. "They'll go away, Ricard, sent back to where they came from, and here in Paris, we'll dance in the streets."

"Is the book any good?" Ricard said.

"It's arty. I prefer a good blue movie."

"So, Kasia, you called."

"Yes, we have the book you wanted—Arthur Koestler, **Scum of the Earth,** it's sixty francs."

Ricard thanked her, and paid for the book.

Ricard left the bookstore and headed for the nearby Café Saint-Germain; the day was dark and drizzling and he needed a coffee. Heading down the street, he heard some kind of commotion behind him, and, as he turned to see what was going on, a running man slammed into him. Both of them fell on the sidewalk. In the distance, shouts of **"Halt!"** and the trills of police whistles. As the man struggled to get to his feet, he mumbled an apology. He was dressed as a worker—baggy, shapeless gray pants and a soiled shirt, but he had the face of an intellectual: a white goatee and spectacles with a cracked lens.

Now, from the direction of the shouts and whistles, a pistol shot, then two more. As the man stood up, the air snapped by Ricard's ear, and his hand flew to his face, but there was no blood—the bullet had missed him. Meanwhile, all around him, people dove flat on the pavement. Up the street, a woman screamed.

The man now took off running and almost made the corner, but a shot knocked him down. Ricard ran to him as he got to his knees and took the man by the elbows to help him up. As he did, the man whispered, "Here, take this," and shoved a folded sheet of notebook paper into Ricard's shirt pocket. Then the man sagged to one side and fell the rest of the way to the street. As Ricard again reached to help him, he saw the life leave the man's eyes; he stared unknowing at the sky.

Ricard ran into the café as a Paris police car skidded to a stop. He sat down at an empty table where the waiter hadn't yet removed a coffee cup and pretended to be just another patron. All around him the crowd spoke in undertones: "Who was he?" "A **résistant**?" Two **flics** entered the café and, using their pads and pencils, began to look at papers and write down names.

The **flic** needed glasses. "Richard?" he said, squinting at Ricard's passport.

"No, Ricard." He immediately regretted the correction; he'd had a chance to keep his name unknown, but his reaction had been instinctive.

"Did you know the man you helped?" the **flic** said.

"No, who was he?"

The **flic** said nothing, and moved on to a woman, hand still pressed to her heart, at the next table. Ricard took the folded paper from his pocket, opened it, and saw what he believed was an engineering schematic with the hand-printed German word **Zünder** and the French word **détonateur**. So, a detonator.

Get rid of it, he thought.

But a dying man had thrust this paper into Ricard's shirt pocket and Ricard couldn't throw it away. In the street outside the café, an ambulance, siren still running, pulled up next to the body. Then a Gestapo officer in a black uniform told the attendants to leave the man alone. A moment later, a Gestapo Mercedes pulled up, and two soldiers hauled the man's body into the backseat, then the car drove away.

Hurrying down the rainswept Rue de Condé, Ricard wore a battered felt hat and a khaki-colored trench coat. At forty, he had a moderately handsome face but was no movie star. Still, women were greatly attracted to him; he was smart and funny and kind, with one particularly appealing feature: he had green eyes, a deep, rich green, knowing eyes, intelligent eyes. He had also a naturally seductive voice, quiet and assured and just deep enough.

At the age of twenty he had left the Sorbonne— he would not become a lawyer or a teacher. His father had died the same year, and his mother, rather too quickly, remarried. Alone and without much money, he decided to do what he wanted, to be a journalist, and found his subjects wherever he could. For example, a recently acquired Velázquez painting, an Adoration of the Magi, was now on exhibition at the Louvre. At the Crêperie Jules, on the Rue de Rennes, some of the best crêpes in Paris, generously stuffed with scrambled eggs and ham. The beloved Hungarian film actress Beáta

Markozy, last seen in **Love for One Night,** was in town to sign a contract for a new movie and was staying at the Hôtel Bristol.

And he haunted the courts: the Delaunay gang of bank robbers captured at last; the widow Robet, who poisoned her husband for his life insurance; the assassination of the Serbian consul in Bordeaux— Balkan politics? No, an **affaire d'amour,** though when the spurned lover went to the guillotine, Ricard stayed home. **That** he did not need to see.

Ricard sold many of his articles to small Parisian weeklies for a few francs, no more. But some of what he witnessed captured his imagination. Not so much the jealous lovers, not so much the scheming postal clerks, not the pistol-waving robbers or the embezzling bank presidents; it was the political crimes that drew his interest. When the poet Azerbajian cried out "Armenia will never die!" as he fired his revolver at the foreign minister, Ricard wanted more. What was the story here? Who were these fiery rebels who gathered at a café in the Seventeenth Arrondissement?

There was, he realized, a novel in this, yes, a detective novel in form but pitched higher, for the sophisticated reader who wanted more than a detective with a cold waiting for a train. Thus, in 1934, a year of Stalinist purges, was born **L'Affaire Odessa, The Odessa Affair,** the hero a minor journalist, Roquette, hunted in the streets of Paris by Soviet secret agents. The cover was lurid—colorful portraits of Roquette, Sauvard of the Deuxième Bureau, the mysterious Ludmila, the secret agent Mischkin. The book sold well; the publisher said, "When may we expect another?"

Ricard had grown up on the Rue des Lombards, in a small apartment that his family could barely afford—it was his mother who had fretted about having a good address. His father had worked six days a week as a clerk in an insurance company, adding columns of figures on an adding machine with a tape—one pressed the numbers one wanted, then pulled a handle on the side of the machine, which produced various clicking noises until the numbers appeared on the tape.

Thus his father was absent during the day, and absent again at night, sitting in his easy chair, absorbed with his newspaper, smoking the daily bowl of tobacco he allowed himself, then holding the unlit pipe in his teeth. Ricard's mother was also absent, busy with what she called "helping friends." How did she help them? By cleaning their apartments? She never would say, deflecting his questions until he no longer asked about her work.

Alone in the afternoon after school, then as a grown man, Ricard walked. Sometimes his eyes discovered a face he wanted to study, sometimes a shop window, displaying things which he would never own. But he hardly cared; what he wanted to do was walk. Perhaps it helped that he was walking in Paris, one of the great places in the world to walk, but Ricard as a boy and then as a man didn't think about that, the monuments—cathedrals, fountains, sculptures of generals on horseback—all this was simply background scenery to Ricard.

So he walked, and became a writer. Because, while walking, his mind was everywhere. In Chicago, in Siam, in a boudoir as a lady undressed, at the circus, on a battleship, in the jungle with a native guide—"Sir! A lion!"—in the snows of Russia as one of Napoleon's Corsican troopers, on New York's Lower East Side with gangsters— "Louie, we gotta rub him out"—at the North Pole with explorers and sled dogs, lost at sea on a sailing ship. Where didn't he go!

Different now. As he walked, Ricard thought about his life, his friends, the women he knew, money—**Too much about money! Think of something else!**—and the occupation, though that thought, like the occupation itself, oppressed him. Still it was **there:** strolling German officers with their French girlfriends, Vichy types with their lapel pins of the Francisque, the double-bladed battle-axe. The sight of such lapel pins inflamed his heart. All his life, Ricard had been a peaceable sort, conflict upset him, but now he would have to fight; he'd avoided, like most Frenchmen, the idea of resistance, avoided it for two years, waiting for rescue, waiting for the Americans, as people put it, but he couldn't wait any longer because it would, in time, damage his soul. No, he told himself, he couldn't just write something hostile about the Germans, he would need to **do** something.

To act.

Heading for a friend's apartment, Ricard took the Filles du Calvaire Métro. The car was packed with Parisians, looking grim and weary after two years of occupation. Nobody spoke, the car was silent, and Ricard was glad to get off at the Pont d'Alma station, also glad that the fierce rain had abated to a sullen drizzle and he could smoke as he walked. He headed quickly up the Avenue Bosquet, staring down at wet leaves plastered to the pavement, past apartment buildings where it cost a fortune to live. Midway up the avenue, he crossed the street to avoid two **flics,** cops, in their black rain capes. All too conscious of the engineering schematic, he didn't want to be stopped and searched, because with the **flics** you never knew; some were loyal to Vichy, some were loyal to France, some were loyal to themselves, so best cross the street.

Just before the avenue met the Rue de Grenelle, Ricard found the apartment building he was looking for. When he rang the bell by the street door, the concierge let him in, her greeting letting him know that she'd seen him often enough to remember him. He took the cage elevator to the fourth

floor, and rang his friend's doorbell. Almost immediately, Romany appeared, in a fitted charcoal-gray
dress—heavily perfumed, perfume bought on the
black market no doubt and even then—alcohol a
designated war material—hard to find.

He said, "Romany," touched her cheek, and she
stepped back so he could get a better look—
she knew the beauty gods had been good to her
that evening. Rumor was that she was Hungarian,
had been born in Budapest to, of course, a family of penniless aristocrats. Asked if this were so,
she waved her hand in dismissal—of Hungarians?
Aristocrats? But Ricard had been with her at a café
a few months earlier, and a well-dressed woman
had stopped briefly at the table, addressed Romany
as **Madame la Baronne,** and ceremoniously lowered her body. Ricard, astonished, said, "Was that
a **curtsy?**"

Romany said, "Poof. Another life," and changed
the subject. Romany was in her forties, maybe, with
light brown hair that fell to her shoulders, and had
some witch in her—all-knowing gaze, mysterious
smile, with laugh lines at the edges of her heavily
made-up eyes. But when she took off her clothes,
and she was good at this, she was a new woman.
She had silky skin, and was shaped like a statue
of a Greek goddess—if the goddess had put on a
few extra pounds. The first time Ricard had seen
her thus he was both surprised and inspired and
they had spent a particularly devilish afternoon in

bed—not for nothing did Romany keep a stack of erotic novels on her night table.

As Ricard closed the door, Romany took his hand and said, "Let's go to the parlor, I'm delighted you telephoned, I needed a visitor today." In the foyer she said, "Hang up your hat and coat, you're soaked."

He followed her down a hallway that led to the parlor. It was a spacious apartment; Ricard sometimes wondered how she'd gotten hold of it— apartments like this were expensive and difficult to find.

She beckoned him to sit on the sofa and, saying, "What filthy weather," inclined her head toward the window, where droplets ran down the glass, while out on the Avenue Bosquet Parisians under black umbrellas hurried through the wet evening.

Romany left the room, returned with two glasses of red wine, gave him one, sat on the other end of the sofa, and said, "Filthy wine, to go with the filthy weather."

"Occupation," he said. "All the good bottles went to Germany."

"And may they choke on it."

He raised his glass, joining her in the toast.

"So, how goes your life, Ricard?"

"Well enough. Like everyone here, I improvise."

"Writing?"

"As always, I just delivered the next. What are you reading?"

She shrugged. "The usual dreadful stuff. In

the 1890s, a young girl comes to Paris from the provinces, you know, filthy men with beards and ankle-length drawers."

"Only men, in this one?"

"Heavens no! In one scene the girl wears a little maid's costume." Romany crossed her arms over her breasts and said, in the voice of a supposedly naïve maid: "Oh, **madame,** we mustn't!"

Ricard laughed, "You do that well."

She sat forward and said, "Ricard, my love, do you have a few extra francs? I'm collecting for Janine, the wife of the neighborhood pastry cook."

Ricard handed over some francs. "What happened to the pastry cook?"

"Shot."

"Any reason?"

Romany raised both shoulders and eyebrows in a brief shrug. "Who knows anymore."

"Romany, I need your help," Ricard said. "You used to, maybe last spring, have a lover who was an army colonel."

Romany's face softened. "Ahh, de Roux, yes, he was for years in the military intelligence, now he's retired to the country, the Vichy generals didn't like him, didn't trust him, thought he was in touch with the English. So now he's gone to his country house, in the village of Les Andelys, on the Seine. You can write him there, Colonel J. P. de Roux, Les Andelys, Eure, will do for an address. Care for another glass?"

"Thank you, I would."

"I'll have one too. It, ah, warms me up, if you know what I mean." She returned with the wine, they touched glasses, drank, and talked for a time. Then she leaned over from her end of the sofa and rested a gentle hand on the side of his face. This gesture, of all that women did, had always reached him more than any other. "I'm cold, Ricard, let's get under the covers."

Ricard spent the night at Romany's. He didn't have a choice, it was two in the morning, well past the eleven o'clock curfew, by the time they'd made all the love they could, but he didn't mind at all, and he slept better with a woman beside him. In the morning, the two went to a café for coffee—"occupation coffee," a few inferior beans with ground chicory added for volume—but at least it was hot. Ricard bought a sheet of paper and an envelope from a **tabac** across the street and wrote Colonel de Roux a brief letter: his old friend Romany had suggested they should meet, so would the colonel be so kind as to telephone him at this number on the fifteenth. The call was set three days in the future, but the French postal service was famously fast, even under the occupation.

Ricard then determined that he had better stop carrying around an incriminating document so took the Métro to the Saint-Michel station and walked up the tiny—too narrow for cars—Rue de la Huchette to his apartment: two small rooms under the roof, a garret, with windows that looked out on the Seine, the Île de la Cité, and the Notre-Dame Cathedral. In one room: a narrow bed, a table that held a well-used Remington typewriter with a French keyboard, a stack of paper, a telephone, and a small radio. By the door stood an impressive walnut armoire next to a small stove that ran on kerosene. His other room was sparsely furnished: an old, sagging sofa, a hideous standing lamp with a lords-and-ladies scene on the shade, and a café ashtray on the floor: the perfect place to read. The garret was very much a sanctuary, where, when storms rolled in from the North Sea, he could hear rain drumming on the slate tiles of the roof.

Ricard took the schematic from the German newspaper and buried it in the middle of his stack of paper.

On 14 October, just after ten in the morning, Julien Montrésor left his umbrella in the urn outside his office and started work for the day. His office, at Éditions Montrésor—Montrésor Publishing—was a small room on the second floor of 9, Rue Jacob, one of the better streets in the Sixth Arrondissement. A few feet away from him sat Madame Anne Legros—war widow, sweet face, heart of gold—his single employee, editor and secretary, who just then gave a gentle sigh of despair and lowered her blue pencil toward a page of manuscript.

As for Montrésor, this was a triumphant morning. Awaiting his attention was the new Paul Ricard novel, a pile of tattered, typewritten pages, its coffee and wine stains, its cigarette burns, testaments to a long journey from desk to café and back again. A detective novel, **Minuit à Trieste—Midnight in Trieste**—from a master of the form, the writer he thought of as the French Eric Ambler, an entertainment, but a smart one, written with a sharp eye and a big heart. The novel was set on a rusty old steamship, the **Rosemarie,** that sailed back and forth between Venice and Trieste in the year 1938. It had been an elegant ship in the 1920s, but the oak paneling in the staterooms was gray with age, the floral carpeting faded, the portholes cloudy, and the smell of the kitchen strong in the passageways as the ship crossed and recrossed the Adriatic, pitching and rolling in the spring storms.

The cast of characters was the usual in such novels: secret police informants, spies, ruined aristocrats, sinister Balkan types, and lithe, exotic women with shadowy pasts. Traveling with them, the hero, the foreign correspondent Claude Verbain, a committed anti-fascist who smoked little cigars and wore tinted eyeglasses. So then, who stole the briefcase from the countess in stateroom 6?

Montrésor was eager to publish this novel. The French, cities blacked out, apartments frigid, rationed food hard to come by, soap a rare treasure, were intent on reading their way through the occupation, the detective novel by far the genre of choice because it took the reader away from the grim reality of daily life. These books were not so easy to find. The first printing sold out immediately, then, secondhand, thirdhand, and beyond, they were bought at the **bouquiniste** stalls on the banks of the Seine as soon as they were put out for sale and, in time, read to pieces.

On the night of 14 October, Ricard attended a **salon** given by his publisher in the wealthy suburb of Neuilly. The house, built of gray cut-stone block, virtually exhaled quiet money, and the room where the reception was held even more so: floors of blonde oak parquet set in dark walnut bands, peach-colored silk draperies, eighteenth-century paintings. Ricard wandered a little, took a glass of champagne, and looked for somebody he knew. That turned out to be the host himself, Julien Montrésor.

"Ah, Ricard, so glad you're here." The voice deep, the words musically fashioned, the smile welcoming. Montrésor wore a certain kind of beard—salt-and-pepper aging toward gray—which crossed his upper lip, passed his mouth, and ended in a square-cut shape below his chin. There was, to Ricard, something Mephistophelian about this beard, as though Montrésor had just ascended to the stage in an opera, the effect heightened by glistening eyes, dark enough to catch the light. Montrésor took his elbow and said, "Lots of writers here tonight, Ricard, sadly not all mine, but let me introduce you around."

Montrésor led him past small groups of men and women in earnest conversation until he found a slim wand of a man with a close-cut beard. "This is Jacques Duchenne. You'll know his book, **Un Homme de la Cité—A Man of the City.**"

They shook hands, and as Montrésor moved away, Duchenne said, "Look at all this, where does the money come from? Surely not Éditions Montrésor."

"You never know, in France, a lot of people have money for all sorts of reasons," Ricard said.

"You're right, there are more than a few whose families got rich in the slave trade."

"Well, it's not like you can't be rich from books— Gaston Gallimard does very well from Proust and Sartre. **Simenon,** for God's sake, he must write a book a week and they sell like crazy."

"Always the same book!" Duchenne whined. "That boring Maigret!"

"But people buy them, it's an addiction."

"Well, I'll never be famous," Duchenne said. "My books are too serious, too intellectual, so I have to spend my life teaching in a lycée . . ."

Before his tale of woe could pick up steam, Montrésor appeared with a tray of champagne glasses. As Ricard and Duchenne exchanged empty glasses for full ones, Montrésor said to Duchenne, "Have you met the journalist Bonaire?

He writes about books for the **Le Matin** newspaper and he's here tonight."

As Duchenne was led away, Ricard met Montrésor's eyes, grateful for the rescue. Ricard then wandered through the crowd, which was getting louder as the wine flowed. Next, Ricard found himself facing a young man with dark curly hair and a dark curly smile. "I know you!" the man said. "You are Paul Ricard, I recognized you from your photograph on the dust jacket. I've read all your books, some of them twice."

"I'm glad you like them."

"I **love** them! Tell me something, what happened to Annabelle?"

Who the fuck is Annabelle? Ricard said, "Umm . . ."

"You know, **Annabelle**, in **Rue Obscure—Shadow Street.** At the end she's going off to meet Michel, does she meet him? Or not?"

"I guess she does, he's her lover, after all."

"**Her lover?** I thought he was her rich uncle. Is she also his lover?"

"Oh yes, of course, I suppose she meets him, but the book ends there, so the reader . . ."

The man leaned closer and spoke in a confidential voice. "Ricard, what's it like, being a spy?"

"I'm not a spy."

The man laughed, an **oh sure** laugh. "How else would you know all that stuff, about the Deuxième Bureau and secret ink?"

"I make it up. I'm a novelist. That's what we do."

The young man was about to get angry when a single note, **ting**, drew their attention to the fireplace, where Montrésor stood holding a knife and a glass. He tapped the glass a second time, and the room grew quiet. "We are privileged to have music tonight. Here is Monsieur Louis Machet, the well-known nightclub violinist, and his accompanists on guitar and bass."

To polite applause from the guests, the three musicians began to play. Machet was a pink-faced gentleman with flowing white hair and wore a printed silk scarf knotted cleverly about his neck. It was easy to imagine him among the tables of a nightclub, serenading the couples seated close together. The trio began to play a version, sentimental and syrupy, of "Begin the Beguine" as the guests paired off and started to dance. Ricard discovered that Madame Anne Legros, the sweet-faced war widow who worked for Éditions Montrésor, was at his side. "Would you care to dance?" he said.

"Yes, thank you, I would," Madame Legros said.

It was a tired old phrase, trite and corny, yet it happened: she melted into his arms. As they danced together, he held her close, felt the warmth of her body, took a step left, then another, and she followed him easily, holding his hand in a way that was both intimate and tender.

"I know this song," he said by her ear. "It's 'Begin the Beguine.' Perhaps we should dance the beguine."

"Do you know how?" she asked.

"No idea."

"Well, we'll do the best we can."

Montrésor appeared from the milling crowd. "Ricard," he said. "Louis-Ferdinand Céline just showed up, I need somebody to talk to him."

"He's a fascist, Montrésor, a Nazi. I want nothing to do with him."

Montrésor sighed and said, "You're sure?"

"A German Nazi is bad enough, but a French Nazi . . ."

Montrésor went off in search of a different guest. Madame Legros said, "Bravo, Ricard," and then the two started dancing again.

Kasia lived in a room above the La Villette stockyards in the Nineteenth Arrondissement; day and night the livestock trucks rattled in from the countryside and cattle cars arrived by rail, the beasts driven down ramps into the pens. At eleven in the morning of the seventeenth, wearing only bra and panties, she sat on the edge of the bed, a cigarette held between her lips, and, squinting through the smoke, worked at loading the clip of her .25-caliber Browning automatic. When she was done, she snapped the clip back in place, then yawned and stretched out on the bed smoking her cigarette and gazing up at the clouds that drifted past her window. She rested an idle hand between her legs and thought about past lovers, brief, exciting scenes that stayed with her. She could think of whomever she wanted, whoever stimulated her, some she'd never spoken to, too bad they didn't know, it might have pleased them. In time, she found herself thinking about a girl she'd seen that morning on the Métro, young, perhaps a secretary, with a soft face and a shag of blonde hair across her forehead. **A little bunny rabbit,** she thought, in need of a stern hand. What would it be like with her? In her imagination she took off the girl's blouse, her skirt, and her bra and panties. Then she touched the girl in a certain spot, between the shoulder and the neck. The girl liked that and let her know it. Maybe, tomorrow morning, Kasia thought, she would take the same Métro.

But first she had to rob a bank. Her eyes wandered to the Browning she'd left on the windowsill. **Pity, now I want to make love but it's not going to be, I'll likely get killed today.** Hah, Kasia! The joke's on you. Here's some bank guard, an old man with his hat down on his ears, and he just made a hole in you, too sad, because you already have all of those you need, this one more is trouble, and why, you silly bitch, are you lying on the marble floor? It's cold down here, and hard, and Jacquot is running away. Jacquot was her partner in crime, a small-time gangster, curly black hair, a knife scar through one eyebrow, a belted, black leather overcoat, big gold watch, gold bracelet, a gangster. **Miserable, mean bastard,** she thought. Running away when she was wounded.

Jacquot—Jacky wanted her. He'd teach her to like men. Old story.

Proud Parisian male, sure of himself, she wouldn't have cared if she never saw him again, but he was a good bank robber, and he was in the **milieu,** the life of crime, and he knew people, people who stole cars, then rented them out to gangsters like Jacquot, people who bought stolen jewelry, people who had hideouts in the city. So she put up with him, let on that his seductive lines amused her.

Suddenly, fast, heavy steps on the stairway. Jacquot. He was coming to collect her. So the bunny rabbit would just have to wait. Work to be done, tra-la, banks to be robbed, tra-la, Kasia to be shot. Tra-la.

Colonel de Roux telephoned Ricard, on the afternoon of the fifteenth, from a **cabinet** at the Bureau de Poste in the village of Les Andelys, raising his voice because it was a long way to Paris. If Ricard would care to come to visit him on the sixteenth, there was a local train, the 2:36 from the Gare de Lyon. The colonel would send somebody to meet him at the station.

This turned out to be a **paysan** wearing a tattered straw hat, sitting on a farm wagon pulled by a skinny nag. Ricard climbed up next to him and, not far from the station, the **paysan** turned onto a **route départementale**—the name for the rough, narrow roads—almost a car and a half in width and

paved with ancient macadam. The road was lined
with plane trees, trunks gray and knotted, crowns
pollarded into round shapes, where the dying leaves
rattled in the autumn breeze. On either side of the
road the wheat had been harvested, leaving fields of
brown stalks lit by the pale blue sky that followed
a rainstorm. As the wagon passed a stone roadside
marker—thirty miles to Rouen—a flock of geese
flew overhead, migrating south in a vee formation,
their honking loud above the quiet fields. It was
famously beautiful here, in what was known as the
Vexin, the Seine Valley: the valleys and hills in a
perfect harmony of land. From time to time the
road ran next to the river, flowing north, its surface
churned by strong currents from yesterday's rain.
A gust of wind sent dead leaves rustling across the
road, and Ricard felt, as the horse clopped along
and one of the wheels squeaked, that he was home,
Paris and its mobs of people left behind; the village of Saint-Denis quickly passed, he was now in
France.

As the **paysan** turned onto a dirt lane, also lined
with plane trees, the horse quickened her pace, she
knew she was home, and, around a gentle curve,
a house appeared. At least a hundred years old.
Colonel de Roux's house, the curved terra-cotta
roof tiles now crooked, the shutters' green paint
flaking away. When the **paysan** pulled up to the

door, some French version of a border collie stood guard, barking at them and prancing about until the colonel appeared and reassured her. The colonel was lean and fit and stood erect, was clean-shaven and had gray hair cut in the military fashion. A retired warrior, Ricard thought, waiting for a call to duty that would never come. After they had shaken hands, Colonel de Roux said, "Welcome, Monsieur Ricard," and showed him into the house.

Inside, the ceilings were low, the furniture well worn, the floors covered with threadbare oriental carpets. Oil portraits of ancestors, many in uniforms long abandoned, hung on the walls. When the colonel had settled in an overstuffed chair, a servant entered the room with a tray of tiny glasses and a bottle of cognac. **"Vive la France,"** the colonel said, raising his glass, and Ricard echoed him. "My friend, Romany," the colonel said, "she is well?"

"Oh, yes, she sends her fondest regards."

The colonel smiled, some nostalgia in his expression, memory of an old and treasured love affair. There followed the necessary prelude—the weather, the house and its peculiarities—then the colonel said, "So then, monsieur, what brings you to my house?"

"I had a strange experience the other day, a man fleeing the police gave me a drawing before he was shot and killed." Ricard drew the engineering schematic from the inside pocket of his jacket.

The colonel found a pair of spectacles on a table

next to his chair, put them on, and peered at the drawing. "A detonator, maybe for a German torpedo, where did it come from?"

"I would guess it was copied at an armaments facility, perhaps in northern Germany, where the workforce is composed of Polish slave laborers. Then it journeyed, I have no idea how, to Paris."

"I can't do anything with this document, Monsieur Ricard, but I think you should. The English will be glad to have it. In war, the smallest thing may be important, crucial, you never know, but getting it to them will not be easy. Still, I can send you in the right direction, to someone in Paris. But I am sure you understand how very dangerous it is for you to be in contact with such people. So, will you take the chance?"

After a moment, Ricard said, "Yes."

The colonel nodded, then stood. "Let's go for a walk, shall we?"

They left the house and walked across a field of wheat stalks; the colonel's dog ran ahead of them, pawing at the brush, sometimes looking back with hypnotic blue eyes. "Nadine is hunting rabbits, she's good at it, perhaps we'll have **lapin** for dinner," the colonel said. "Tell me, monsieur, did you serve in the military?"

"I was too young for the Great War, but in 1940 I was called up in May, sent to an infantry unit fighting near Soissons on the river Aisne. We had old Lebel rifles, the Model 1886, for the year of manufacture, so . . . we did the best we could."

"**Le Débâcle** we call it now," the colonel said, "everything went wrong, nobody really responsible, which is the worst merde of course. The politicians fought each other all during the thirties, fighter planes weren't built, tanks were manufactured without radios, the tanks at least had treads, but the fuel trucks didn't, now Paris is full of German tourists."

"We held our own," Ricard continued, "fighting on the river, old rifles and all, we never ran away. But then, the Panzer tanks appeared, the Blitzkrieg went right through us. My unit surrendered, they had us marching up some road, but, at nightfall, I took a walk."

"Ah yes, the famous Blitzkrieg, lightning war, unstoppable. A Goebbels invention, that idea. The Germans **had** to win quickly, because they didn't have gasoline for their tanks. Wehrmacht truck drivers were allowed only ten days' practice. These boys came from the country, most had never driven anything, so now they're trying to drive trucks on Russian roads."

"What will happen there, do you think?"

A rabbit came scooting out of the brush, Nadine in close pursuit, but the rabbit found a hole and disappeared. The dog stood there, staring at the hole, then turned to look inquisitively at her master: **Where did it go?**

"The Russians will destroy the Wehrmacht—too many Russians, many are killed but more appear. It's the same with tanks and warplanes. Hitler is deluded; the Germans don't know it yet, but they'll find out."

When Ricard and the colonel reached a hedgerow that bordered the colonel's property, they turned around and walked back to the house. After another cognac, the colonel said, "Why don't you stay for dinner? We'll eat early and you'll just make the 9:07 back to Paris."

"Thank you," Ricard said.

"It will be good to have company. Now, it's come time for me to help you with your diagram. But, please, everything I tell you is in confidence."

"Naturally. One thing the occupation has taught me is to keep my mouth shut."

The colonel nodded with approval. "There is a café, the Café Albert on the Rue Saint-Dominique in the Seventh Arrondissement: at four in the afternoon, approach the barman—it is the proprietor, Albert, who works that shift—and tell him you are seeking one Monsieur Duval, then sit down and wait; this may take some time. Eventually, you will be given a contact, likely an address where you will be put in touch with the people who will know what to do with your diagram. I would strongly suggest that when you enter the café you take a good look around—the Gestapo is known to be active in that **quartier,** drawn by the wealth and status of the arrondissement's population."

"I will be careful, Colonel."

"Now, dinner, can you smell it?"

"I can."

"Beef stew with potatoes and carrots, a specialty of my cook, especially since the occupation. At least you won't have to use your ration coupons. We don't eat so badly out in the countryside, especially when an old cow dies."

17 October. His instructions from the colonel would have him at the Café Albert at four in the afternoon, so Ricard decided to make himself work for two hours, then leave for his rendezvous at three-thirty. He glanced at his watch, a few minutes after eleven. **Get busy,** he told himself, **because this book won't write itself.** Ricard had a writer's fantasy based on "The Sorcerer's Apprentice," where an enchanted broom sweeps the floor by itself. Perhaps, if he spoke the words of a magic spell, his typewriter would write his new novel while he watched. He stared at the Remington, but it just sat there. With an unvoiced sigh, he squared up his stack of blank paper, adjusted the position of his typewriter, and aligned two sharp pencils.

Now where was he? He always started his novels by writing an outline, which was supposed to spell out the entire book, but his effort never lasted longer than fifty pages. Still, he had to try. Working title: **The Investigator.** On his bookshelf there was the autobiography of a Parisian arson investigator, written in the 1930s. Many stories, and much technical description. So then, his new hero would be an arson investigator. Ricard named him Valois.

Valois is a confidential agent, a private detective, whose specialty is arson, and who works for insurance companies. In Paris? No, in Switzerland, in Zurich! That said **insurance company** to Ricard. A suspicious fire has burned down a factory. Where? In France? No, a more foreign sort of place. Maybe . . . Bucharest. Good. Valois would be sent, by his hardheaded despot of a boss, who always, at first, scoffs at Valois's theories, to Bucharest. So he will go to Roumania on—what else?—the Orient Express.

Now, he would need a romance.

Ricard lit a cigarette, sat back in his chair, and gazed out the window for inspiration. **Maybe,** he thought, the larcenous rascal who'd burned down his factory would have . . . a wife? A much-younger wife? No, Valois was an honorable fellow, he wouldn't sneak around, he wouldn't chase wives. A lover? No, the same but worse. Give the factory owner a daughter, then. Who lived at home and took care of the household. Not, on the surface, a beauty. She would be educated, she would be—he hunted for the word—**prim.** He liked that word: **prim.** So, put her hair up in a bun, put her in eyeglasses, give her compressed, disapproving lips, the shape of her body unknowable in the severe suits she wears.

So, how would he seduce her? Ah, much better,

he wouldn't, **she** would seduce him, afraid that he knows the truth and Papa will be arrested. At least that is what she tells herself; in fact she has wanted Valois from the moment she first saw him.

TRAP!

What to do with Papa? Let him go? Not in Ricard's detective novels or anyone else's. So then, kill him. Ricard had killed off inconvenient characters for his whole career, but it had to be their own damn fault, their insatiable greed would prove their undoing, so **au'voir.** Satisfied, for the moment, with his outline, Ricard found himself musing over his night with Romany, was tempted to lie down on his bed for a while. However, he had to work, so sat forward and returned to his outline.

Four in the afternoon. Ricard entered the Café Albert on the Rue Saint-Dominique and found it busy and loud. He looked at the patrons, as he'd been instructed to do by the colonel, but at first saw nobody who might have been a Gestapo officer in civilian clothes. Well, there was one, sitting at a table with an **apéritif,** who didn't belong, but the Gestapo always traveled in pairs, and this cold-faced gentleman was alone.

Ricard waited at the bar until the barman—Albert the proprietor according to the colonel—came to see what he wanted. He ordered a beer, and wondered if Monsieur Duval had been in yet. He saw the recognition in Albert's expression, then the proprietor said, "Your friend is waiting for you, at a toy shop called Le Petit Soldat on the Rue des Récollets, just across from the Gare de l'Est railway station. The shop is closed, but the door will be left open for you."

The toy shop was indeed closed, the interior dark and still, but intact. There were shelves of soldiers, dolls and dollhouses, toy trains with stations and locomotive drivers, and more, all beautifully crafted in fine detail, made of tin and wood, while the soldiers were molded in lead. There were yo-yos, paddleball sets, wooden puzzles, and stuffed animals.

In a shadowed corner of the store Ricard saw a striking woman: thirtyish and dark with a gently curved nose and eyes almost black. She comes, Ricard thought, from the eastern Mediterranean, from Turkey perhaps. Stylish and poised, she wore a slate-gray raincoat and tight, shiny black gloves with gold buttons at the wrist, she could have, then and there, posed for the cover of a fashion magazine. Saying "Bonsoir, monsieur," she moved toward him, and shook hands, the hand inside her glove warm and firm.

"Bonsoir, madame."

She smiled to put him at ease and said, her voice low and husky, "Thank you for coming to meet me, would you please tell me your name?"

"Paul Ricard. And you are . . . ?"

"I am called Leila."

Leila, he thought. Perhaps a false name, perhaps not, but the sound of her name touched his heart.

She took from her pocket a sheet of stationery and a fountain pen, wrote down his name, then said, "I am told you are seeking to make contact with us."

"Yes, that's right. I was instructed to approach a fellow at a bar, he sent me here."

"And can you tell me who instructed you, Monsieur Ricard?"

"A French military officer."

"And his name was?"

"I'll just leave it at that." He smiled, she smiled. This was a spy game, rules had to be obeyed.

"Very well," she said. "And what is your work?"

"I am a writer of detective novels."

Now she smiled; this news interested her. "Titled, for example?"

"Oh, **L'Affaire Odessa,** for one."

"And where do you reside?"

"On the Rue de la Huchette, number nine."

"Well," she said, "now that you've made contact, how can we help you?"

"I was given a certain document, there's nothing I can do with it myself, but I believe it might be useful to certain people in London."

"May I see it?"

Ricard took the schematic drawing from his pocket and handed it to her.

"How do you come to have this?" She emphasized the word **you.**

"A man, fleeing from the police, was shot down in front of me. As I tried to help him, he put this paper in my pocket. Then he died."

"And how much shall we pay you for it?"

Ricard felt slightly affronted. "I don't want anything."

Leila was pleased, nodded to herself; this wasn't an **x** transaction, this was a **y** transaction. "Then perhaps we'll be in touch with you, perhaps you might help us."

"I will. Whatever you need, just ask. You have my telephone number?"

"Yes, I have it."

"Then you'll call me."

She met his eyes, then nodded slowly, saying, "Soon."

"Does someone own this toy store?" Ricard said.

"Owned by Jews, at one time. They fled, if they were lucky. Or they were taken away."

"Who ever thought that such a thing would happen," Ricard said.

"There were those who did," Leila said. "Throughout the thirties. Some of us knew, but nobody would listen to us."

"Sad," Ricard said.

"It is," Leila said. "I will see you again, Monsieur Ricard."

"Whenever you like," Ricard said.

She left the store, walking quickly, turned up the street, and disappeared.

In Paris, the last day of October was a treasure: a bright sun, white wisps of cirrus cloud strung across the sky, and, all over the city, people were in a good mood, the commonplace exchanges of Parisian life—**excuse me, you're welcome;** the elaborate, **remercier** version of **thank you**—delivered with intimacy and warmth. At nine the previous night, Ricard had listened to the French program of the BBC, volume down because you would be shot if they caught you doing it: the U.S. Marines were fighting on Guadalcanal, the British making headway toward El Alamein, the Germans again repulsed before Stalingrad.

In his garret, Ricard looked out the window at the busy life of the Rue de la Huchette—so much in Paris happened in the street. On the **terrasse** of the Café La Régence the tables were all occupied, a formally dressed older man was buying flowers, bargaining, but not too hard, for a dozen red gladioli, kids in short pants were playing soccer with a ball made of old rags, shouting at each other as they ran. In time, Ricard forced himself back to work. **Do you like writing?** he was asked quite often. A difficult question. He hated hard work, and writing was very hard work, at least for him. A shrug and I **can't really do anything else** usually sufficed.

At that moment, he was toying with the character Valois, the arson investigator, in his novel **The Investigator.** He put a mustache on him, then took it off, then put it back. A **shaggy** mustache, he thought. Valois was his own man, good enough at his job to dress as he liked and say what he wanted. Tightly wired heroes weren't much in evidence in Ricard's detective fiction.

And then, the Bucharest problem—Ricard had never been there, so time for the Guide Bleu and Fodor's **On the Continent.** A lucky photograph of a tram showed it painted red and yellow. He then installed yellow wicker seats—if some finicky reader knew different, well, too bad.

The telephone rang. People often disconnected their phones because the Gestapo could use them as microphones and hear everything you said, but Ricard disliked being cut off from the world and so kept his plugged in. He put the receiver to his ear and heard a woman's voice, fraught with anxiety. "Oh, Paul, it's your friend Leila, there's something I need to discuss with you. I'm in the station buffet at the Gare du Nord, waiting for a train, but the train's late, so we'll have time to talk."

"I'll be right there."

2 November, 1942.

At ten-thirty in the morning, Kasia changed into a moss-green sweater and slacks beneath a raincoat.

She tried putting the Browning automatic in her pocket, but it made the coat sag, so she put it in the waistband of her slacks. Then she rode her bicycle to a branch of the Banque du Commerce on the Avenue Hoche, a block from the Courcelles Métro. She began locking her bicycle to a lamppost a little way from the bank, taking her time and looking busy while she waited for Jacquot and his friend Antek. Ten minutes later, walking fast, they arrived.

Kasia entered the building first, her job was to reconnoiter the bank and make sure nothing was different than on a previous visit. The bank guard was the same one as before: a stoop-shouldered little man with gray hair, a holstered pistol at his waist— likely not cleaned for years, she thought—shifting his weight as, hands behind his back, he stood to one side of the vault. Kasia approached the high counter, got change for a fifty-franc note, then left. Her reappearance was the signal for action, and she followed Jacquot and Antek into the bank.

Trouble right away. As Jacquot shouted, "Hands up! Nobody move!" the bank guard drew his pistol and fired at Jacquot, missed him, but hit Antek in the foot. Antek cried out and began to hop back toward the entry. Then the guard aimed at Kasia but hesitated, possibly reluctant to shoot a woman. Such chivalry cost him dearly, as Kasia shot him twice in the thigh. Jacquot grabbed the back of her overcoat and yelled, "Get out!" Turning to leave,

Kasia found herself facing one of the tellers, terrified, scream stifled by a hand over her mouth. It was Paulette, last name forgotten, a former schoolmate at Kasia's lycée. Now Kasia was truly in the merde, and she swore as she ran for her bicycle. Up the street, Jacquot was helping Antek into a taxi. She doubted the driver would forget them, and Paulette certainly wouldn't forget her.

The waiting room at the Gare du Nord was crowded when Ricard arrived, the station buffet in one corner was busy, with people waiting to be served. Lost souls, with nowhere to go, nursed their coffees and read old newspapers they'd found left on the benches. Fugitive couples, trying not to be noticed, leaned toward each other in whispered conspiracy. Some of the people in the waiting room, headed to the countryside in search of food, held rolled-up burlap sacks and ancient valises, to be filled with potatoes, turnips, and carrots. Among the other travelers on the wooden benches, families leaving occupied Paris for occupied Lyons, hoping that life would be better there. Wehrmacht officers smoked and relaxed, knowing that the first-class carriages were reserved for them. Well-dressed businessmen checked their watches, fearing that their trains would be late. They feared also a train so overcrowded that the stationmaster would order it to leave early.

Despite the crowd, Leila, in her slate-gray

raincoat and black leather gloves, was easy to spot. Ricard got a coffee and sat down next to her on the bench. "Very public place you chose for a meeting," he said.

"They told me I had to see you right away. It seems that your drawing has caused a great stir."

"Well, I'm glad to be rid of it."

"I think maybe they are not done with you. They asked me to give you this."

This turned out to be a cinema ticket, a balcony seat for the following evening's showing of **Les Visiteurs du Soir—The Night Visitors,** a fifteenth-century costume drama, directed by Marcel Carné and starring Arletty, with Jules Berry as the devil. "Have you seen it?" Leila said.

"I wasn't sure I'd like it."

"Well, now you'll find out."

Wehrmacht major Erhard Geisler, properly SS Geisler, woke at seven-thirty, reached out to stroke his mistress—sometimes she could be coaxed into lovemaking before breakfast—but found only a note on the dent in her pillow. "Sweetheart, I have early work this morning. See you tonight." The message was signed "Kiki," her signature followed by abundant X's and O's. Kiki was originally from Alsace and, before moving to Paris, worked as a stenographer at one of the numberless bureaux that administered the occupation of France.

Geisler's suite at the luxurious Hôtel Crillon—the

Germans had taken all the best hotels in Paris as their barracks—had two large armoires, and Gerhard opened one of them and stared at the neat row of suits. **What to wear today?** He had a choice: Civilian dress or uniform? In civilian dress he very much blended into the crowd: a pear-shaped fellow in his forties, bland and colorless, with clear plastic-framed eyeglasses. Had he been in the Gestapo, he would have had to wear the uniform, but he worked for the SD, the Sicherheitsdienst, the intelligence service of the Nazi party, and so could wear whatever pleased him.

Well, not really. This morning he had a meeting: representatives of all the German security services would have yet another discussion about the suppression of the French Resistance, and everyone would be in uniform. So would he, but he didn't mind so much. His black SS uniform fit perfectly, well sewn by one of the Jewish tailors in German concentration camps, where all German uniforms were made.

From a row of shoes at the bottom of the armoire, he chose the well-shined black pair that accompanied his uniform. Geisler had a refined taste in shoes, having once worked as a salesman at a shoe store in Düsseldorf. That was in the bad old days, before he joined the Nazi party. He had a low, thus early, registration number, had joined up with Hitler in the 1920s, and this fact helped him in the eternal power struggles that went on in high party circles.

Now life went better. He made lists, using the endless stream of reports and denunciations that reached him from all over France, but particularly in Paris, where the citizens especially loathed the Germans and the occupation. From these lists he made other lists, and these unlucky people were arrested, interrogated, and sent on to concentration camps, or executed immediately. But Geisler never did any of this himself; he was what was known as a **Schreibtischmörder,** a desk-murderer: a pale, insignificant man, but deadly.

His job now, in occupied Paris, followed a certain doctrine, an old and honored tactic of those who occupied nations other than their own: Control the Culture. The Wehrmacht occupied France, now the French had to be taught to think in a new way. So, to control the culture, he needed the people who worked in that culture: journalists, radiobroadcasters, teachers, and writers. He had asked his secretary, a bright-eyed young lieutenant, to prepare a list, and on that list was the entry: **Ricard, Paul J., Detective Novelist.**

The following evening, Ricard attended a showing of **The Night Visitors,** using the ticket for a seat in the balcony that Leila had given him. Before the occupation, Ricard had liked sitting in the balcony, where it was dark and intimate, but no more. Now the houselights were left on, by order of the Germans.

Early in the occupation, the audience had been demonstrative once the theatre went dark and the newsreel, produced by the German propaganda department, came on the screen. Demonstrative was barely the word. From the audience, on those evenings, Hitler's appearance in the newsreel was greeted with a great barrage of oral farts, some loud and extended, others brief and sibilant, you couldn't find a public toilet in France with more variety. Meanwhile, on the screen, from a confident, smiling Hitler, a quote from yesterday's speech. "We are winning the war," said the subtitle. And a particularly loud chorus of flatulence had greeted that news. So the Germans decreed that the houselights must stay on. A very unwelcome decree to those who liked to kiss and hug at the movies. To the French, the Germans were harsh and relentless, but they were also very annoying.

As Ricard climbed to the well-lit balcony he thought, **Theatres should not be seen in the light.** The red cushions of the seats were stained and soiled, the carpeting on the floor no better—in some places ripped and sewn back together—and bore, beneath the seats, torn shreds of paper and old ticket stubs that the cleaners had ignored. An usher read his ticket stub, pointed out a vacant seat, and, a few minutes later, the newsreel began: German tanks crossing a bridge, girls in peasant costumes dancing in Wiesbaden. Then, leading another patron behind him, the usher beckoned

Ricard to follow, climbed the stairs to the projection booth, and knocked on the door, which opened to admit Ricard and the other patron, who handed the projectionist a few banknotes folded together and nodded toward the door. Now the two of them were alone in the darkened booth, the unattended projector clattering away on its table.

The other patron said, "You are Monsieur Paul Ricard?"

"Yes, and you are?"

"A friend of your friends in London, I am known as Teodor."

He spoke almost but not quite as a native Parisian, in an educated voice with, perhaps, a faint note of Eastern Europe in his accent. He wore a powder-blue double-breasted suit, a half size too large for him, and was clean-shaven, had strings of colorless hair plastered across his scalp, sunken cheeks, and crooked teeth. He seemed, to Ricard, obsequious, like a headwaiter seeking a generous tip.

"Monsieur Ricard," he said, "you are a writer—is that correct? I believe I may have read a book of yours. **A Season for War,** did you write that?"

"I did."

"It was very good, I thought, the intrigue especially. Do you have some practical experience in that area? Working as a spy?"

"None at all."

"Well, here's your chance to get some. The

people—civil servants, we'll call them—in London, who received the engineering schematic, need your help, urgently need it. They want more information: Who is doing this? Who got this to Paris? What are their names? How can they be contacted? Is it a Resistance cell? To the people in London, that would be a real treasure. You see, Ricard, you've struck a nerve. The detonator in your diagram is to be used in a torpedo, and the torpedo, once installed in a German U-boat, is meant to destroy merchant shipping, many lives lost, important cargo burned up or sunk. So you can't blame the British for . . . pursuing the source of this. Wherever that drawing came from, there's more to be discovered: maybe technology the British don't know about, maybe people, Poles or others, who can help the British war effort. Do you see what I mean?"

"Yes," Ricard said.

"I would be lying if I said it wasn't dangerous—here you enter Gestapo country. I know you are a French writer, now you have a chance to be a French patriot."

Ricard nodded and waited for more.

"You must begin with your friend Kasia; are you her lover? How did you meet her?"

"I am not her lover, she works with a gangster called Jacquot, who is a bank robber."

"Well, when it comes to fighting Nazis, nobody cares what Jacquot does for a living. But first comes Kasia."

"I met her in the bookstore where she works," Ricard said. "A small bookstore, on the Rue de Condé, just off the Rue des Écoles, close to the Sorbonne, so there are always students around. On the shelves, Sartre, Camus, all the existentialists, and plenty of books by radicals—of the left, of course. Kasia and I somehow hit it off, we liked each other, she's a free spirit, you know, a tough Polish kid."

"Well, it sounds to me as though she would be willing to do more."

The man who called himself Teodor paused, took a cigarette from his pocket, lit it, and shook out the wooden match. "You'll have whatever help you need. Somewhere, a long way west of this balcony, you will find the bombed city of London, where, whistling as they climb over the rubble on their way to work, are certain British civil servants, who have offices with obscure titles on their doors. They have, like the rest of their class, the most amiable and polite exteriors, but the work they do is secret, and often cruel. And the war, which at the moment Britain is losing, has made them desperate, so there is not much they won't do. Really, nothing they won't do. Now Hitler, in that lump of coal he calls a heart, believes he is fighting 'a nation of shopkeepers.'" From Teodor, a brief and very cold laugh. When he continued, he said simply, "He is wrong."

On the screen, the wandering minstrel Gilles was seducing the innocent ingenue Anne, while the devil, who wanted Anne for himself, watched from behind a drape. But then, in a close-up, the devil turned yellow, then brown, and started to disappear altogether, all this accompanied by the smell of burning acetate and whistles and offended shouts from the audience. Teodor quickly adjusted a lever on the side of the projector, and the movie began again.

As the film continued, Ricard said, "Of course I **could** try to get what these people want, but it would involve going to Germany, and first I would have to obtain press credentials, a travel permit to cross the border, and I would need a **reason** to go."

Teodor crushed out his cigarette on the floor of the projection booth and lit another. "What is your opinion of the Vichy government?"

"They are traitors. Loathsome creatures, I have nothing but contempt for them—any honorable Frenchman would say the same thing."

Teodor nodded. Yes, he agreed. But the nod meant more—it acknowledged that what he had heard from Ricard was what he wanted to hear. "Dreadful people," he said. "Many are fascists, but most are opportunists, who would do anything to rise above their competitors now that the game has changed. Of course the Reich courts the Vichy sympathizers, treats them as friends, allies in the struggle for Europe. To get into Germany you could pretend to be one of them."

"Why me, Teodor? I'm just a detective novelist."

"Not quite. You are now Kasia's handler, as the civil servants put it. So you are stuck with the job and, as a French patriot, you'll do it well."

Ricard hesitated, then agreed, with, as the French put it, **un petit oui,** a little yes.

"Good, Ricard. You'll have help, the civil servants have a lot of money and a lot of friends, so you are not without resources. Go and serve the honor of your country."

3 November. The morning after the robbery, Paulette, the teller at the Banque du Commerce who'd seen Kasia shoot the guard, was troubled from the moment she awoke. Turning to look at her husband, she saw that he was also awake. He was a mean, pompous man, a traveling salesman who sold dry goods in the Paris region. She said, "Pierre," then the story came tumbling out in a rush.

"Are you sure?"

"Yes, I'm sure. I knew her at lycée."

"And so, what do you intend to do about it?"

"What could I do?"

"Inform the authorities, **ma douce.**"

"You can't mean . . . denounce her?"

"You must, it is your civic duty to do so."

"I owe the Boche nothing."

"Well, it is more what they will owe us, a thousand francs for this information, I would think."

"Please, I beg you, Pierre, don't make me do such a thing."

"What if she's arrested and interrogated? What if they find out you recognized her? What then, eh? I'll tell you, then you'll be in the soup."

"You are telling me to go to the Boche?"

"Yes. We'll go together, to the occupation people at the Hôtel Majestic."

Paulette resisted for a time, but eventually she agreed—Pierre was her husband, and one had to obey one's husband. Thus it happened that at dawn on the fifth of November, a squad of detectives, led by a German officer in civilian clothes, kicked in the door of Kasia's room. The **flics** knew where she lived, because the **flics** knew where everyone lived.

Kasia sat bolt upright in bed as the lock gave way and the door flew open. She thought about reaching for her Browning, but it was wrapped in oiled paper and hidden at the bottom of a dead houseplant on her windowsill. The **flics** searched her room, but they never found it. They told her to get dressed, watched with interest as she did so, then pulled her hands behind her back and snapped handcuffs on her wrists.

They took her to the massive Fresnes prison, south of Paris, where she was locked in a cell with three other women. One of them was a young **résistante** who had been caught leaving propaganda leaflets on the Métro, one had fled with her lover, a chauffeur who had stolen jewelry from his employer, and the last was a prostitute called Olga, who had slapped an official when he'd demanded something she didn't like to do.

It was she who befriended Kasia, who was in a bad way, facing years in prison for bank robbery. This was not the first time Kasia had been on the edge of catastrophe, and she had always managed to escape the final blow. But now she was never free from tears. Olga was a good soul, sometimes at night would climb to the upper berth of the bunk and crawl in beside her, would hold and stroke her and tell her everything would work out. On occasion the sympathy went beyond comfort, but this lovemaking was Kasia's preference, and she responded eagerly.

Absolute silence was the rule at Fresnes for most of the day, but in the hours they were allowed to talk, Kasia told her cellmates some of her story. She had, in fact, been in jail before: eight months in a Bulgarian prison in Sofia, and five months at Antalya in Turkey. But now she faced a trial in the indefinite future to be followed by time in prison. She had had no word from Jacquot, who she thought was in hiding, having escaped with the wounded Antek from the bank robbery. Bad luck for Kasia that her old friend had been working at the bank, bad luck that Paulette had denounced her. Fate, she thought, it would find you.

But then . . .

"Prisoner 45042, come to the bars." This from the wardress, in her blue uniform.

Kasia did as she was told.

The wardress inserted a key in the barred cell door and let Kasia out into the passageway. "You have a visitor," she said, and led Kasia to the small room with a table and two chairs where visits took place. Kasia sat on the prisoner's side of the table and waited, then a seedy man entered the room and sat across from her. He was not an appealing individual; he had sunken cheeks, strings of hair plastered across his head, and crooked teeth.

"I brought you a tin of sardines and an orange," he said. "The guard has them." He had, Kasia thought, a slight Balkan inflection in his speech.

"Thank you, monsieur."

Teodor paused, then said, "Would you like to leave this place, Kasia?"

"More than anything in the world. Who are you, monsieur, a lawyer?"

The answer to this question was oblique, based on the probability that conversation in this room was being secretly recorded. "No, I am not a lawyer. My friends call me Teodor, and we have need of someone who speaks Polish. There is travel involved, would you mind?"

"It doesn't matter, just tell me what to do."

"That will come later. For the moment, expect a visit from a lawyer in a day or two. You will be released, probably at night, and I'll be waiting for you outside the gates with a car."

Kasia wanted to kiss his hand, an ancient peasant instinct that she resisted. "Thank you," she said. "Thank you, Teodor." Kasia had never felt such a surge of gratitude. At this point Teodor left the visiting room. As she was led back to her cell, Kasia asked the wardress about the tin of sardines and the orange, but the woman just shrugged.

That evening, Teodor met with Ricard, who had been directed, at the Café Albert, to a garage in the industrial suburb of Saint-Denis. It was a chilly, windless evening, with dry flakes of snow drifting down over the city, a thin slice of moon visible when the clouds parted. Ricard waited in the unlit garage, which reeked of gasoline and had the cold, dead air of a place that had never been heated. A third of the garage had been isolated by floor-to-ceiling wire mesh, with an ice-blue Bugatti sports car parked behind the wire. To Ricard, it looked like the car was in prison. After the Germans had occupied the country, they took all the cars, especially the fancy ones. Thus wise owners had hidden their automobiles; the writer Simenon famously parking his in a barn.

On the surface, Ricard was calm, a man doing what had to be done. He truly hated the loud, strutting Germans, and wanted to strike a blow against them. But in his heart what he really wanted was to run away—he'd been trapped, trapped by what now seemed a foolish desire to help the war effort. **Idiot,** he thought, **naïve idiot.** Why had he not understood that, in these times, the idealist would pay a stiff price. With a caustic eye, he looked back at Ricard the writer, who should have kept intrigue confined to paper. Now he was lost, moving down a labyrinth he didn't understand. But it was too late; this was no plot that could be revised; this was his reality and he hated it.

There was a door next to the shuttered entry to the garage and, a few minutes into Ricard's sermon to himself, the door opened and Teodor appeared. This was the clandestine Teodor, wearing an overcoat with the fur collar turned up and a hat tilted low to obscure his face. "Ricard," he said. "Good that you are on time."

Politely, Ricard said, "Bonsoir," as though they were two acquaintances who had just happened to meet in a deserted garage.

"The civil servants in London," Teodor said, "have for years kept close watch on the French press and they have a suggestion for you. Do you know the newspaper called **Le Journal du Jour?**"

"Alas, I do. In the thirties, when the right and left were tearing each other apart, the **Journal** was worse than most. If a left-wing senator proposed money to improve the railroads, the **Journal** attacked. They called him a Stalinist. And blood, according to the **Journal,** dripped from his Bolshevik fangs."

"The foreign editor at the **Journal** is a Monsieur Lagache," Teodor said. "He will approve whatever you propose to do because he's been reached—as the Russians put it, he is **nasch,** 'ours.' Once you have an assignment in Germany, you must next get a travel permit from the Propagandastaffel at the Hôtel Majestic. Of course you will be interviewed, and you will reveal your Vichyite sympathies.

"In all probability, the man you'll see at the Propagandastaffel is called von Lobau, Major von Lobau. He is one of those Germans who, following the victory in 1940, pulled strings to get a job in Paris. He is enchanted with Paris, was a tourist here before the war. You know the German expression 'God lives in Paris'? Well, von Lobau is a believer in Paris; the dingiest workers' cafés, the **clochards** with their bundles of rags, the smallest restaurant— **Mère** this, **Chez** that, where they serve every innard known to beasts, where you can smell piss on the pig's kidney you're served, von Lobau loves it all."

"He doesn't sound so bad," Ricard said. "Among tourists, it's a point of pride to have experienced the 'real' Paris."

"Well, Paris won't be the subject of your story for the **Journal,** that subject will be somewhere in northern Germany, close to the city of Kiel, where the Germans build their U-boats, using Polish laborers. Once you find your way there, you can begin to investigate, you can begin to make contact with the Poles who work there, and you will, if you are lucky and don't get caught by the authorities, find the source of your drawing and work to get more."

Ricard thought it over, then said, "There is one difficulty, Teodor, I don't speak Polish."

"That eventuality has been foreseen," Teodor said, with some satisfaction. "Your friend Kasia will accompany you and act as your interpreter."

At Teodor's direction, Ricard went to see Lagache, the foreign editor of **Le Journal du Jour,** at his office on the Rue de Richelieu. It was a small, cramped office, on the shadowed side of the courtyard, with framed newspaper photographs on the walls: mostly well-dressed men shaking hands, radiant actresses with their escorts, and a few glum criminals being led away by detectives.

Lagache had a dark complexion, with a thin nose flanked by small eyes set close together and a mouth which had sneered so often that the twisted smile lived permanently on his face. He had a pencil line of a mustache, eyeglasses with thick frames, and wore the Vichy emblem, the Francisque, the double-headed axe, on a lapel pin. Sitting across from him, Ricard felt palpable hatred flowing across the desk. According to Teodor, Lagache had been fixed, bribed, but that didn't stop him from loathing his enemies—one of his greatest pleasures. Like the rest of the world, Ricard was no stranger to being disliked, it happened; still, Lagache's withering glare made him uncomfortable.

As a fascist, Lagache was a fervent believer in the Vichy regime, thus a disciple of the white-mustached General Pétain, the leader of the French right wing, who claimed that the fall of France was due to the corruption of the true French values: family, work, and religion. The followers of Pétain's enemy, General de Gaulle, were accused of drinking too much wine, eating too much fine food, and making too much love. Pétain would have called them libertines; Ricard called them French.

After hating Ricard for a time, Lagache drew a gold fountain pen from his desk set, unscrewed the cap, affixed it to the end of the pen, and said, "So then, Ricard, where is it you wish to go?" The absence of the **monsieur** title was an insult, but Ricard didn't care.

"I am going to Lübeck, in Germany," Ricard said. He knew the city of Lübeck was forty miles from the U-boat facilities in Kiel.

"And what news event will you be covering?"

The civil servants in London had an immense and very private library in an anonymous office building near the Mayfair district. Here they had every newspaper and journal published in the principal cities of the world, as well as books of a political nature, and it was one of their librarians who had suggested an assignment for Ricard.

"A new bridge has been built across the river Trave," Ricard said. "It is to be called the Heinrich Himmler Brücke, and the opening ceremonies will take place on the fifteenth of November."

Lagache wrote a few more words, then put the cap back on his gold fountain pen. Ricard could see that this was, to Lagache, a symbolic gesture: power had spoken. Lagache then called to his secretary, seated just outside his office. Following the clackety-clack of her typewriter, Ricard had his assignment letter, on official **Le Journal du Jour** stationery, in an unsealed envelope. He rose to say goodby but drew from Lagache only a final, and particularly intense, glare. It wasn't simply emotion, Ricard thought, it was a threat: When Germany wins this war, we will settle with you and your Gaullist friends.

His assignment letter in hand, Ricard went off to keep his appointment with Major von Lobau, the German bureaucrat who loved Paris, at the Hôtel Majestic on the Avenue Kléber, at the ceremonial center of the city, within sight of the Arc de Triomphe. The hotel was the nerve center of the occupation, high-ranking German officials streamed in and out of the guarded doors as their Grosser Mercedes automobiles, military drivers in attendance, stood waiting on the avenue.

About von Lobau, Teodor had been cautionary. "He cannot be bribed," he'd said. "He will have to be manipulated. And though he will be wearing an army uniform, he in fact works for the SD, the Sicherheitsdienst, the **real** German intelligence service, the lawyer Schellenberg and his pack of fellow lawyers, who have nothing to do with those brutes in the Gestapo."

Von Lobau's office was on an upper floor, isolated from the busy offices that managed the occupation. A sign on the door said PROPAGANDASTAFFEL, a brass plate next to it, MAJOR F. J. VON LOBAU. When von Lobau's orderly admitted him, Ricard entered a room that reflected the tastes of its occupant: this was not an office where plans for slaughter were issued, but the workplace of a sophisticated and intelligent administrator. Von Lobau awaited him at a low table on the other side of the room from his desk, where a coffee service—delicate china cups and saucers, dainty little silver spoons—had been set out.

"Will you take a coffee?" von Lobau said.

"Thank you, I will," Ricard replied.

"One lump or two?" von Lobau said.

Ricard took two, sipped the coffee, and found it perfect, prewar coffee, the real thing.

Von Lobau was a distinctive-looking gentleman. In his thirties, he had light blond hair, heavy lips, and pale, almost colorless eyes, with just the faintest touch of blue for color. He could have been, Ricard thought, from the far north of Europe, maybe Estonia, somewhere up there, put armor on him, give him a staff with a pennant, and you would have a Baltic knight of an earlier century.

As Ricard sipped his coffee, the orderly entered the room and handed von Lobau a dossier, a stiff, green cardboard folder. **My dossier!** Ricard thought. **There it is!** This was something one never expected to see. It was packed with typewritten papers, some of them stapled together, and copies, flimsies, of issued documents. **Merde, what's in there?** Likely memoranda—**We believe that subject RICARD,** or **On the night of 9 August**—perhaps information taken from his neighbors—**We're not sure of her name, but she**—or from his concierge, his former teachers, friends, lovers past and present. Von Lobau, his face without expression, opened the file and skimmed through the pages. As he read, he took a pencil in hand and idly tapped the eraser on the wood surface of his desk. Eventually he looked up from the dossier and said, "May I see your assignment letter, Monsieur Ricard?"

Von Lobau scanned the letter quickly, then said, "Vichy seems to approve of your work."

To this opening, Ricard merely nodded.

"One would think you were on the side of General de Gaulle; I mean, from your books, one would think that, no?"

"Yes, one would," Ricard said.

"But not now? You've changed sides? Had a political conversion?"

"Not really. I no longer have a side. You know Mercutio's line, from **Romeo and Juliet,** 'A plague on both your houses'? That is what I've come to. French political opinion was so complex and combative—both sides fought among themselves

as much as they fought each other—then some-
time in the 1930s I gave up on it. I would glance at
the front page of the newspaper, shake my head in
despair, then proceed to the soccer. That at least I
understood."

This was utter bullshit, but von Lobau didn't
care. It was his job, the power he had, that caused
supplicants to make up stories they thought would
work. Now he turned back a few more pages in the
dossier and said, "So, Monsieur Ricard, I see you
are returning to journalism, any reason for that?"

"Books take a long time to write, and the money
is slow in coming, so I spoke with an editor at **Le
Journal du Jour** and was assigned a newspaper
story."

"The dedication of a new bridge in Lübeck. Will
that be an interesting subject for you?"

"One more human story, the world goes on,
and I saw how I could make it good reading.
Ceremonies have their own stories: there will
be folk dancers—chubby girls in dirndls—and
mayors wearing their official sashes, automobiles
waiting on either side of the bridge, seeking the
honor of being the first one to cross the new span,
tugboats decorated with crepe paper blowing their
steam whistles . . . and if I do this well there will be
another article in the future."

"Well, I see I must give you permission. And I
will look forward to reading what you write."

"Thank you, Major von Lobau."

"And when you return, you might consider occasional visits to my office, there will always be coffee, or something stronger, and we might discuss where you've been and who you've met. Journalists turn up everywhere, they encounter all sorts of people and situations that one would like to hear about. It is the mission of this office—one of them, anyhow—to gain insight into French life, especially Parisian life. One can always use some extra money, and we would be pleased to help you out there. Our relationship would of course be confidential, most confidential, you may assure yourself of that."

This was no time to insult a powerful officer, so Ricard pretended to consider the offer, then said, "Thank you, Major von Lobau, I will certainly think it over." **No.**

From his desk drawer, von Lobau took various forms, filled them out, then applied this rubber stamp and that rubber stamp. "So you're off to the dedication. I'm sure you will enjoy the folk dancing, the young maidens in their dirndls and the lederhosen, and be thoughtful about what you say on the subject of Germany. You wouldn't want to hurt my feelings, would you."

Of the thousands and thousands of secrets in Paris, Madame de la Boissière's private shop was one worth knowing. In her forties, she had bright blonde hair, thin lips, and eager, restless eyes. Once upon a time she had married an aristocrat, who gambled away his fortune at the tables in Monte Carlo, then, classically, went into the garden and shot himself. This left his widow with a spacious apartment at the far end of the Jardin du Luxembourg, a multitude of rich friends, and no money. She had, however, a Parisian woman's feel for style, began to buy friends' clothing when they no longer wanted it, and soon had, standing wall to wall in her apartment, racks of beautifully tailored suits and dresses from fine little shops.

For their trip into Germany, Ricard needed a new version of Kasia. So, off to Madame de la Boissière. Who took one look at Kasia in her worker's cap and pea jacket and said, "I have the very thing! She will be **bon bourgeois** in an hour."

She was true to her word. Kasia stripped down to bra and panties, Madame de la Boissière stared as she did it, then took her firmly by the shoulders, turned her around, placed a firm hand across her bottom and held it there as she said, "You have a sweet ass, dear." Kasia turned her head around and smiled at the compliment, then curved her back so that her bottom stood out for Madame de la Boissière to admire. Then Madame de la Boissière held up outfits for her to see, and soon enough moleskin trousers and ankle-high boots were replaced by a cream-colored shirt, a brown wool suit, and tie-up oxford shoes with chunky heels.

Kasia was delighted with her new look, stood at the mirror, turned to see one profile, then another, and was clearly pleased. Three days later, Paul Ricard and Kasia, his translator, at 10:08 in the morning, boarded the Paris-Brussels Express, headed, after a change of trains, for Lübeck, forty miles from the submarine base at Kiel.

12 November. In the rain, under a low, dark sky, chaos. Half the crowd around the Gare du Nord surged toward the station; the other half headed for home. This was not the same madness that struck every year on the first day of August, when almost all Paris headed away from the city at the same time, intent on not losing a minute of their August vacation. But this was November, where was everybody going? **Away.** Occupied Paris was claustrophobic and difficult, so any excuse would do: **Let's go see Tante Renée in Tours.**

Because of the coal shortage, only a few trains were running, and they were mobbed; travelers packed the aisle that ran past the compartments. On the platforms, children were towed along by their parents, travelers ran to make their trains, couples hung on to each other in the mêlée, and the use of sharp elbows was common. As for the German soldiers among the crowd, space magically appeared before them.

At last, after struggling to hear the staticky PA system, and having tried several platforms, Ricard and Kasia reached the train for Brussels. Ricard had meant to buy tickets for the express train, but these were long reserved, so it would be first class on the local. Eventually, Ricard and Kasia found their compartment, gratefully sank onto the faded red-plush seats, and lit cigarettes of relief. Outside the grimy window, faces appeared—somebody searching for somebody—then vanished. As travelers found their seats, they immediately raised the windows to continue saying goodby to those who had accompanied them to the station. Traffic on the platform was slowed by those passengers who never got on a train without asking the conductor where it was going.

Finally, the conductors called out **"Tous à bord!"** and travelers lingering on the platform hurried to climb the steps into the railcar. Ricard and Kasia thought they might have the compartment to themselves, but, when the locomotive hissed as it vented steam, two Wehrmacht troopers entered the compartment, stowed their rifles, helmets, and heavy duffel bags above their seats, and politely greeted Kasia and Ricard. These were German combat soldiers—officers always took the express, even if a few poor souls had to be kicked off the train to make room for them. The troopers wore **Feldgrau**—field gray—uniforms, with ribbons and medals pinned to their tunics. Likely they had fought in the army that defeated France in 1940, had been assigned to occupation duty in one of the northern towns, then given furloughs in Paris before they went off to fight in Russia, fifteen hundred miles away.

One of the soldiers took out photographs he'd had developed in Paris and showed them to his friend, who said, "Is that Sylvie?" Even with the subject upside down from where he sat, Ricard could see a plump redhead with a crooked smile.

"That's her, in front of the bar in Pigalle."

"Here's one of her friend."

"Mimi."

"Yes, with the big tits."

"God, I was drunk."

"They didn't care, they like soldiers."

Soon enough, the troopers fell asleep, so Kasia and Ricard whispered to each other. "Merde, it is **triste** here," Kasia said, staring out the window. She wasn't wrong. Headed for Brussels, the track ran northeast of Paris—flat fields in the November rain with only an occasional village, and soon enough the names of the towns were the names of the Great War battlefields—Amiens, Arras, Cambrai— this was, after all, Flanders, "the cockpit of Europe," where armies had fought since the Middle Ages, killing each other with everything from crossbows to rifles. One Flemish farmer, turning over the earth in his field, had revealed a line of twelve bayonets—a squad caught in battle order as they moved down a trench and died, frozen in place, of a shell concussion. Outside the train window, a field of white crosses that took the train a long time to pass.

"Nobody comes here, do they," Kasia said.

"The French know what happened here, they don't like to think about it. When Parisians get rich enough to buy a country house, they look west of Paris, near Rambouillet or Chevreuse. Too many bad memories here, an uncle dead in 1914, a brother a year later. The artillery barrages went on for days—they fired a million shells. Still, when the French troops went over the top, German machine guns were waiting for them. Day after day after day, until the mutinies in 1918. Then the generals executed their own troops."

Kasia said nothing, lit a cigarette, and watched the fields go by.

The local train never went much over thirty miles an hour, stopping at stations only a few miles apart, village stations, serving villages on roads that for centuries had been reached by horse or foot, the roads still flanked by very old plane trees. Ricard said, "We had better go and have something to eat," and the two went off to the dining car. The SNCF—Société Nationale des Chemins de Fer Français—had done the best it could: pale green canned peas in a thin mayonnaise, a two-egg omelet with scallions, four pieces of bread in a straw basket, and a battered pear with one bad bruise. Ricard and Kasia were grateful for whatever was served, finished everything, then went back to their compartment. They were almost dozing, heard only the clatter of the train wheels, but the German troopers' hearing had been sharpened in battle, and they both woke up suddenly. "**Scheiss!**" one of them said.

His companion pulled up the window, stuck his head out, and looked up at the sky. Only now did Kasia and Ricard become aware of a low, droning sound somewhere behind the train, a drone that became louder each second. "What is it?" Ricard said.

The trooper replied in German and Kasia translated. "It is the RAF, the British bomb this line."

Suddenly, the train sped up. "What's he doing?" Ricard said.

The trooper looking out the window said, "He's trying for a tunnel ahead of us, he can hide the locomotive under there."

Two bombs straddled the train, sending fountains of dirt into the air and blowing window glass into the compartment. Then the train stopped with a screech of air brakes. The trooper said, "The engineer has got the locomotive under the tunnel."

Ricard touched a place beneath his eye, extracted a small shard of glass stuck in his cheek, dabbed at the blood with his handkerchief, then began to brush shattered glass off his trousers. From one of the cars ahead of them, a passenger dove out of a window, then rolled into a ditch by the side of the track.

The British plane was a dive-bomber, and the pilot, having dropped both of his bombs, now began to strafe the train from end to end.

Bullets punctured the roof above Ricard's compartment. An orange tracer round penetrated the roof and passed on through the floor, leaving a hole in the wood and a wisp of brown smoke that curled up in the air. On his way back down the train, the British pilot saw the man hiding in the ditch, fired his machine guns, and the man stood up, then sat down and tilted slowly backward.

One of the German troopers retrieved his rifle, put a round in the breech, leaned out the window, and tried for a shot at the bomber. "Horst!" his companion said. "Don't make him mad!" and Horst sat back down.

As the drone of the bomber's engine faded away, it was replaced by a quiet, rainy afternoon. From the edge of the field, crows called out as they flew above the trees. Some of the passengers left the train, as did Kasia and Ricard. Up ahead of them, where the train's engine had stopped under the tunnel, the engineer stumbled out of his cab and sat on the embankment that supported the tracks, one hand held to his heart. A small spaniel had gotten away from its master and ran, barking hysterically, across the field. One of the passengers approached a conductor and said, "We have a dead woman in our compartment."

"Which car were you in?" the conductor said. The passenger told him and the conductor replied, "I'll bring a blanket and we'll cover her up . . . that's all we can do until we reach Brussels."

It was two-thirty in the afternoon with a slow, steady rain and low cloud that darkened the sky until the train stood in twilight. The engineer—a conductor supporting him with an arm around his waist—returned to his cab and restarted the locomotive. Then, as the train gathered speed, a second British bomber appeared, first as a dot in the sky, then an airplane, losing altitude as it descended toward the railroad track.

At that moment, the train was chugging around a long curve, and Ricard could see the cars ahead of him. He saw the first bomb miss, landing far to the left of the train, but on his second run the British pilot improved his aim, and a bomb fell next to the coal car behind the locomotive. Ricard saw its right-side wheels rise into the air, then the car fell on its side, crashing down the embankment and spilling its coal. But the coupling held, causing the passenger car next in line to go over as well. Then the locomotive fell, spewing steam in the air as it lay on its side while the engineer scrambled out the window and jumped to the ground. Meanwhile, the following passenger cars tilted over, and tumbled down the embankment.

Ricard, stunned, found himself lying on top of Kasia, the two troopers sprawled next to them. From a nearby car, a woman screamed. Ricard managed to get to his feet, then said, "Are you alright?" Kasia raised her hands and, gently, Ricard helped her to her feet. She looked down at the jacket of her new suit, which had survived intact, but Kasia brushed at it anyhow, saying, "Those bastards, don't they know we're on their side?"

"They don't worry about that, they're ordered to bomb a certain train and that's what they do." Ricard now reached up and tried to open the window above his head, but it wouldn't budge. Standing next to him, the trooper called Horst said, "Cover your eyes," and, with the butt of his rifle, broke the window, careful to smash out the glass at the window's edge. Next he told Ricard to cup his hands. He put his foot on them and thrust himself upward through the broken window. Then he lay flat on the side of the upturned railcar and reached inside. "The woman first," he said.

Kasia was easy to lift. Briefcase in hand, she slid down the side of the car, stood in the field, and lit a cigarette. When Ricard had climbed through the window, he joined her. "What happens now?" she asked. As passengers left the train, they sat on the embankment, grateful to be alive. After an hour, on the far horizon, a convoy of gray-green trucks appeared, then stopped. "Ah, the Wehrmacht arrives," Horst said. Ricard helped Kasia to her feet and they, among dozens of other passengers, began trudging across the field toward the trucks.

On the night of 12 November, Ricard and Kasia wandered around Amsterdam, looking for a place to stay—their train to Hamburg would leave on the morning of the thirteenth. But the city was busy, the hotels packed with Germans on leave. All they could find was a hotel room in Die Wallen, the brothel district, where naked women sat behind windows in rooms painted red and lit by red light. In Ricard and Kasia's room was a single bed they could share, a wooden stool, and a lone bulb hanging from the ceiling on a cord. The madam who showed them to the room had grown fat a long time ago and wore a loosely tied floral-print wrap. Eager for company, she invited them up to her apartment, where she produced two quart bottles of beer with ceramic plugs and three water glasses. "Where are you two coming from?" she said.

"Paris," Ricard said.

"Ah, Paris," she said, with a nostalgic smile. "What's it like, these days?"

"Occupied, but not too bad. The Boche want to keep it a playground for their troops on leave, so all the cinemas are open and, if you can afford it, there's good food to be had. Still, Germans everywhere."

"Don't like 'em?"

"Not much."

Having established that the two shared her feelings for the Germans, she said, "Do you like to listen to the radio?"

Ricard said they did.

"What time is it?" she said.

Ricard looked at his watch and said, "Almost nine o'clock."

"Nine o'clock is always a good time to listen to the radio."

This took Ricard a moment to decipher, and it was Kasia who said, "You mean the BBC, don't you."

"I do, sweetheart, I never miss it, I can get the French service here."

She lumbered over to a small Emerson radio next to a fern in a pot and began to fuss with the dial. In a few minutes, they heard the four opening notes of Beethoven's Fifth Symphony—dot-dot-dot-dash, Morse code for V as in "V for Victory"—that signaled the BBC broadcast. The announcer's voice was smooth and unemotional, the news itself hopeful, as though, Ricard thought, the war had begun to turn—one notch, no more—in the Allies' favor.

The lead story: German forces had now occupied all of France—an acknowledgment that France would never be Germany's friendly neighbor, as the Germans had foolishly hoped. Next, British and American troops had invaded North Africa, landing on the beaches of Morocco and Algeria, heading for Casablanca, Algiers, and the Algerian city of Oran.

From there, Ricard knew, they could launch an invasion of Mussolini's Italy. Churchill, in a speech on the radio, had said, "This is not the end. This is not even the beginning of the end. But it is, perhaps, the end of the beginning." All in Churchill's deep, rumbling, and fiercely inspiring voice. In the Pacific, American marines had invaded the island of Guadalcanal, meaning to take the Japanese-built airstrip. Meanwhile, the Wehrmacht, fighting in waist-high frozen snow, could not break through the Russian lines that defended Stalingrad.

When the broadcast ended, the madam of the Amsterdam brothel, with a broad smile on her fleshy face, raised her glass of beer and said, "To victory, my friends." Ricard and Kasia repeated the toast. Not long afterward, they returned to their room, stripped down to their underwear, and crawled into the narrow bed—so narrow that the only way they could both fit on the lumpy mattress was to lie on their sides, Kasia tight against Ricard's back, her arm wrapped around his chest, the heat of her body warming his skin.

Because it was dark in the room, and silent in the blacked-out street, Kasia spoke in a whisper. "What train do we take tomorrow?"

"The 2:08 from Central Station. We'll be in Emden by six or so."

"Emden?"

"The border post between Holland and Germany. Then we go on to Lübeck."

"In Germany."

"That's where it is, my love."

She was silent for a moment. "Do you worry, about being in Germany?"

"Yes."

"But you go."

"Yes."

"Why?"

Ricard laughed. "It's a long story."

"What will they do to us if we're caught?"

"Throw us in jail. For starters. But I have an assignment letter, and permission from the Propagandastaffel."

"It will work?"

Ricard shrugged. "I believe it will."

She brooded over this, then tightened her arm around Ricard's chest. "I'm frightened, Ricard. I don't show it, we Poles don't, we expect each other to be brave . . . but I've been in prison."

Ricard reached back and pulled her closer. "We're not going to be arrested, Kasia. For what? Our papers are good, we haven't done anything wrong."

She nodded, felt better, and, not long after, her breathing changed and she twitched and muttered in her sleep, kicked him once, then quieted down.

VOYAGE
TO THE
REICH

AT THE BORDER POST IN EMDEN, DUSK WITH NIGHT fast closing in. The rain had stopped and there were faded red streaks amid the dark clouds. A light wind toyed with the red-and-black swastika flags, and the passengers, leaving the train for document control, knew they were in Germany now, so they didn't say much, or spoke in undertones. A kind of hush, on the German side of Emden, where guards in Wehrmacht uniform watched the passengers carefully while their Alsatian shepherds strained at their leads: chains attached to broad leather collars. They had been trained to attack civilians and they wanted to do it.

Ricard and Kasia stood patiently on the long line, eventually reaching a junior officer who took their documents in hand. He was young, nineteen or twenty, likely a former member of the Hitlerjugend, the Nazi youth program which one entered at the age of fourteen. He certainly had the Aryan look: tall and pale with steel-framed eyeglasses. Slapping Ricard's passport against his upturned palm, he said, "What brings you to the Reich?" The **you** was accented, as though Ricard's mere existence was offensive.

"I am writing an article for a French newspaper," Ricard said.

"You have a permit from the Propagandastaffel?"

"Yes, sir."

The officer didn't like Ricard. "Let's see it," he said.

As Ricard rummaged through his briefcase, the officer rested his hand on the butt of his holstered pistol, ready to arrest Ricard, wanting to arrest him. Ricard found the letter and started to give it to the officer, but there was an interruption. A senior officer appeared from the customs shed with a mousy little fellow held by the collar of his jacket and hauled upward, so that he had to walk on his toes. Then the officer shouted at his subordinate, "Klebner! What are you doing, Klebner? How did this little **Arschloch**—asshole—get past you? He's a smuggler, Klebner, he's got a suitcase full of stockings. **Silk** stockings!" The officer's face was red with anger, smuggling provocative clothing for women was worse than just smuggling.

Klebner, a pink flush of shame on his cheeks, apologized to his superior. Taking hold of the man's shoulders, he spun him around, manacled his wrists, and began to march him away. The man, his voice high and pleading, said, "But sir, I am just a simple salesman."

Kasia began to whisper something to Ricard, but the officer yelled, "And you, you shut your mouth."

Klebner, with his prisoner halfway to a waiting van, turned and gave Ricard a look of pure hatred. The officer who'd yelled at Klebner took Ricard's papers, stamped them, and waved him through. As Ricard and Kasia walked over the border and headed for the train to Hamburg, Kasia said, "You're lucky today, Ricard, that was almost the end of you. He would have found something 'irregular' with your permits. He intended to arrest you."

Slowly, Ricard's pounding heart settled down. "I know," he said.

They boarded the train and found a compartment in the second-class carriage. Ricard opened the window—the night air was chilly and damp—then watched as other passengers trudged along the platform, suitcases in hand. They didn't speak. Turning to Kasia, Ricard said, "Kasia, why is it so quiet here?"

"The Germans are afraid," she said. "They go to

sleep afraid and they wake up afraid. That's Hitler and his Gestapo at work. That's the way they want it. They like fear."

Ricard felt his anger return. "Hitler. Why doesn't somebody . . . ?"

Kasia crossed his lips with her finger. "Don't," she said.

In Lübeck, a bright, windy day at the river Trave, a banner hailing the new Heinrich Himmler Brücke snapped in the breeze, and the local dignitaries, sashes crossed from shoulder to waist, held on to their hats. In the crowd were wounded veterans of the Wehrmacht, one of them legless, seated on a wheeled trolley that he drove with gloved hands. Also in the crowd: local women, who held tin cans, rattled the coins inside, and asked for donations to the **Winterhilfe,** which sent warm clothing to the soldiers fighting on the Russian front.

The RAF had bombed Lübeck seven months earlier, destroying the historic center of the city and damaging the bridge, which had now been repaired. Thus the ceremony proceeded much as Ricard had imagined it would. A speech by a dignitary. Followed by another speech by another dignitary. The crowd applauded enthusiastically. Then it was time for the oompah band and the chubby maidens in their dirndls, folk-dancing girls who slapped thighs and shoulders in time to the music.

As the dance ended, and the mayor of Lübeck approached one of the ceremonial banners with a giant scissors made of cardboard, a single-engine airplane passed overhead. The crowd looked up, saw no threat, but went silent until the plane flew over. Then the mayor—with the aid of a town clerk using a real scissors—cut the ribbon, and the crowd cheered.

16 November. In the morning, Ricard and Kasia had coffee in a little breakfast room in the basement of their hotel. When their coffees were served, they sipped at their cups and lit cigarettes. "So today," Ricard said, "we take a branch-line train to Altona, which is joined to the city of Hamburg, and from there we go up to Kiel."

"Have you ever been to Kiel?"

"No, but I know about it. It's a major port on the Baltic Sea—the U-boat pens are in Kiel, so that's where somebody copied the engineering schematic, some Polish laborer at a workshop in one of the navy yards."

For a moment, Kasia was thoughtful. "Do you think they will let us anywhere near the docks?"

"I promise they won't, we'll have to find another way—the Poles are forced to work there, but they come back to some sort of camp at night, so we can look for a place where they gather to drink." Ricard glanced at his watch and said, "Time to leave for our train."

•

In Altona, Ricard and Kasia found the railway station near the center of the town, learned that their train would leave in an hour, and settled in the waiting room. Kasia said, "Can't we find a railway timetable? That would make life easier."

"It would, before the war they were in every station. But the Germans don't want the RAF to know the train schedule, so the timetables disappeared."

In the waiting room: sailors and officers of the Kriegsmarine—the German navy—looking smart in their well-tailored dark blue uniforms, as well as the usual crowd of weary travelers sitting by their suitcases. Also in the crowd, two men, in their thirties, perhaps, wearing civilian suits and gray felt hats. These two struck Ricard as slightly unusual— men in Germany were typically in uniform—but perhaps these two were officials of some sort, headed up to Kiel on state business. They didn't have briefcases, however, and they weren't reading newspapers or talking. And, on closer inspection, they weren't really the "official" type. They could have been soldiers, big guys with hard faces, but they looked more like policemen. Like detectives.

"You're watching the two over there?" Kasia said.

"I was trying to do it covertly."

"You weren't succeeding, and in a minute they're going to come over here and say hello."

Ricard looked down at his shoes. "How's this?"

"Much smarter. You were staring at secret police, and secret police don't like to be stared at."

On a chalkboard at the front of the waiting room, a station worker wrote that the train for Kiel would be delayed. "Merde," Kasia said. "Maybe it's been bombed."

"Some train will show up," Ricard said. "They have to keep the railways running."

"Excuse me, sir." In the aisle that ran past the bench where Ricard was sitting, a young man with carefully combed reddish-blond hair and a bright smile held an unlit cigarette in his lips. "Have you a light?" he said.

Ricard took a small box of wooden matches from his pocket and lit the man's cigarette. "Thank you," he said. "Going up to Kiel together, are we?" He wasn't precisely rude; more overfamiliar, his tone knowing and smug.

"We are," Ricard said. "We were in Lübeck, for a story about the Trave River bridge, and we thought we'd walk around Kiel for a while. Maybe have lunch."

"It's an interesting city, Kiel; our Baltic fleet is based there, as it's at the foot of a long canal, merchant shipping can steam down from the sea, but the storms stay where they belong, over the open water. Do you have friends there? If you tell me their names, I might know them, I know so many nice people in Kiel."

After a moment, Ricard said, "I don't believe we know anybody in Kiel," his tone softly defiant. **Agent provocateur,** he thought.

"And what about you, young lady, perhaps you have a friend or two."

"I don't," Kasia said shortly. This intrusive man was getting on her nerves, and, she sensed, he was threatening her behind his bright smile.

"Well, maybe we'll run into each other. It's a small world, as they say."

"It is," Ricard said. **Go away.**

"Then I wish you a good afternoon," the man said, and walked toward the back of the waiting room.

"One more secret agent," Kasia said. "This place is crawling with them."

"He surely wanted us to know what he was."

"Oh, yes, he's all technique," Kasia said sourly. "I am done with this country, Ricard, I want to go back to Paris, where I belong."

Just then, their train was announced, and the two found an empty compartment. As they waited for the train to depart, there was a tap-tap on the window, and Kasia looked out to see the young man with reddish hair waving to them. He then moved away, up the platform, headed for a different carriage.

Two hours later they were in Kiel. At the station, the usual border guards had been replaced by

SS men, in their black uniforms and silver skull insignia. It was their presence itself that was threatening, they wanted to get you alone somewhere. Just at that moment they had to serve as border guards, but they had business with you and they would finish it. Ricard and Kasia parried them with courtesy until the guards produced their document stamp. Ricard and Kasia left the station, relieved that they hadn't been arrested, but then, two blocks further on, they were stopped at another control, this one supervised by detectives in civilian suits. No stamp this time, only long and careful looks. A few poor souls were taken out of line and searched, but Ricard and Kasia were not among them. After the two had been permitted to pass, Kasia said, "I have a bad feeling, Ricard, let's go home."

"Not yet, we have a job to do here. We should at least have a look at the port."

They followed Feldstrasse until the tall cranes of the port came into view, then turned right and found themselves on the broad street that ran along the waterfront. Here and there a wharf had burned to blackened timbers, while two cargo ships, half sunk and floating on their sides, rose and fell with the current. Across the street, some of the warehouses had been bombed out, their brick façades spilled out into the street.

Even so, the port was busy. Freighters were docked in a long row, some of their names were Scandinavian, some Spanish, some Portuguese—

ships of neutral countries. Along the wharf, tall cranes bearing nets, worked by stevedores, were loading and unloading cargo. On the tops of the buildings across the street from the wharves, anti-aircraft positions, Bofors guns, manned by gunners and servers in circular tin helmets.

At the far end of the street was a row of bars, ready for the workers when they got off shift. "Let's try one of the bars," Ricard said. "Maybe somebody knows where the Poles are kept." As they headed for the bars, they saw a small ferry landing with a sign bolted to a piling. Here, departure times for ferries to Norway, Denmark, and Sweden. **Occupied Denmark,** Ricard thought. **Occupied Norway. Neutral Sweden.**

Walking past the bars, Ricard said, "Look, here's one for the dockworkers." The bar was called Das Haken, the Hook, and painted on a wooden sign above the door was a longshoreman's steel hook with a wooden handle. As the two entered, conversation stopped while the patrons, in workmen's clothes with tweed caps, stared at them. **Strangers.**

Ricard and Kasia stood by the end of the bar near the door. In time, the barman had to acknowledge them. "Yes?" he said. "What can I get for you?"

"Beer," Ricard said. "For my friend as well."

The barman drew two beers from a tap, then brushed the foam off the top with a wooden stick. As he finished, Ricard said, "Any Polish bars around here?"

The barman stared at him.

"My friend here is Polish, and looking for her brother, who was working as a stevedore."

"Can't help you," the barman said. Clearly, strangers asking questions weren't welcome at Das Haken.

Ricard and Kasia left the bar and headed up the street. They hadn't gone far when one of the bar's patrons, an older man with a seamed face and hands knotted by a lifetime of handling cargo, came trotting after them. As he caught up he said, "Keep walking." They took a few steps, then he said, "That sonofabitch wouldn't help you if you were on fire. There **are** Poles here, the Nazis rounded them up and brought them to Kiel and forced them to work. They're machinists, tool-and-die men, welders, electricians, and there **is** a place where they gather, a sort of bar, in an old workshop down an alley behind a warehouse on Kieler Schloss street. It's owned by a man called Jozef, but there's no name on the door." After Ricard thanked him, the old man said, "Be careful, comrades, this isn't a good place to ask questions." He took a step back toward the bar, then turned and raised a stiff arm with a closed fist—the international communist salute.

By now, the sun had set and dusk was closing in. On the wharves work continued, winches straining and grinding, warning whistles sharp in the air as cargo nets swung between the freighters and the dock. A splintering crash caught Ricard's attention: a crate had slipped from its net and fallen to the dock, spilling out newly manufactured rifles wrapped in oiled paper. "They feed the war here," Ricard said.

Kasia nodded and said, "They do, and, if it ever ends, they will start another."

They walked for a time, both of them squinting up at the street signs in the twilight. Finally, the Kieler Schloss. The warehouse here had been hit in the bombing; some of its windows had been blown out, there were scorch marks flared out on the wall below them, and the air smelled of old fire. The building's door was boarded up, and there was a handwritten sign on a piece of cardboard nailed to a board:

**HOFMANN UND SCHULTZ
CUSTOMS BROKERAGE
IMPORT / EXPORT
(FORMERLY SZAPERA AND GOLDMANN)**

Behind the warehouse, a narrow alley where a tar-paved walkway led to an abandoned machine shop, a shack with a rusted tin roof. Ricard knocked and the door opened to reveal a room lit by two candles, with a dirt floor, and six rough-carpentered tables with benches. Along with the smell of stale cigarette smoke, a faint scent of burned metal. Two men sat on one of the benches holding shot

glasses of vodka, a third stood, serving as bartender.
Jozef's Bar.

Kasia greeted them in Polish, and they responded.
Then the man behind the table said, "Would you
care for a vodka?"

"We would, thank you," Kasia said.

"You come here from Poland?"

"From France, up in Lille, where the Polish
miners work."

Jozef nodded and poured out two shot glasses
of vodka. Kasia raised her glass and said, "**Na
zdrowie!**" To your health. The men repeated the
toast, as did Ricard.

"Very good. What shall we pay you?"

"Two sous a glass."

"Very reasonable, my friend."

"Well, I make it myself."

When Ricard drank off his vodka, it burned like
fire, all the way down.

"Have one with us?" Kasia said.

"Don't mind if I do."

Jozef poured the shots from a thick glass bottle
with no label. Once again, "**Na zdrowie!**" Kasia
spoke French to Ricard, and he paid for the drinks.

"I was wondering . . . ," Kasia said in Polish. "A
friend of mine got a letter, it came by hand, all the
way to Paris. We're not sure who wrote it, maybe
someone who works over here, but it made us
curious."

"Us?"

"My friend Ricard here, and me. I'm called Kasia."

"He's maybe an . . . official?" By way of not saying **policeman**.

Kasia laughed. "Him? No, no. He's just a friend of mine from Paris. He writes books."

She knew this would hit home; Poles greatly admired intellectuals. "Then you're welcome here," Jozef said in French.

Kasia said in Polish: "This letter was about his work, whoever wrote the letter, his work building submarines."

Jozef turned to his friends. "Do we know anybody like that?"

The men shook their heads, but Jozef met Ricard's eyes, and Ricard immediately understood that it had been he who had copied the schematic.

"Perhaps," Ricard said, "if you discover who it was, you can find a way to let me know." He produced a small pad, tore out a page, and wrote down his address on the Rue de la Huchette. From somewhere outside, the mournful call of a ship's horn sounded three times.

"What's that?" Ricard said.

"Come outside, you can hear it better."

When the three stood in the walkway, the sound was repeated.

"Kriegsmarine ships," Jozef said, "putting out to sea."

"Jozef," Ricard said, "how do you come to be here?"

In the moonlight, they could see a rueful smile. Jozef was of medium height, wore a tight beard, his wire-frame spectacles bent slightly out of shape. He had a strong, thereby handsome, face, with a determined forehead beneath a receding hairline. He could have been, Ricard thought, an intellectual, something of the professor in the way he looked—a professor in a former life. Ricard lit a cigarette and gave one to Jozef.

"There are about thirty of us here, we were all taken prisoner during the invasion of France. The Germans shot the intellectuals—potential leaders—but they missed me, for some reason. I told them I was an electrician. Actually I had taught economics at the University of Cracow."

"Yet you persuaded them that you were a real electrician."

"I worked next to a real one, he showed me how to do the wiring. Anyhow, in time they took the technicians and put us to work out here. In the beginning, they treated us badly, but the work slowed down, so they gave us some freedom— that's how I came to have the bar."

"I thought 'forced labor' meant barbed wire, guards with truncheons, prisoners worked to death," Ricard said.

"It does mean that, but not here. Here there are skilled technicians, too important to the German war effort to control with such brutalities—they **need** us. So we don't live in barracks behind barbed wire, they put us in an old school, abandoned a long time ago. We don't have much heat, but we gather coal on the railroad tracks, some always falls off the coal cars."

"What happened to the Germans who used to work here?"

"In Russia, freezing to death at Stalingrad. There are tens of thousands of Frenchmen working in Germany, taking their places, Belgians, Dutchmen, Poles—Europe is part of the German empire now. For how long I don't know, but it's like the last war, we wait for the Americans to show up."

"Tell me, Jozef," Ricard said, "is there someplace we can stay in Kiel?"

"You've seen the bars along the wharf, try there. They often have an empty room on the second floor, and they let people spend the night for a few reichsmarks."

Walking back along the tar-paved path, Kasia said, "They must know here when the German ships sail, isn't that valuable information?"

"It's something," Ricard answered. "But if somebody knew what ships they were, that would be **very** valuable. I'll pass along the information."

Jozef served a final vodka to his patrons, then, at ten in the evening, he closed the bar and locked the door. A sharp wind blew onshore from the canal, which meant rain would follow, but weather was not going to keep him from his evening retreat.

As usual, he walked away from the waterfront and climbed a high hill. From the crest, beneath a near-full moon and a starlit, cloudless sky, the Kiel Canal was easily visible, its water calm and black. Glancing at a pocket watch he had bought from a friend, he saw that he had a few minutes before he had to return to the school. He didn't want to be caught breaking curfew. The Polish workers were tightly guarded by a Ukrainian SS unit, teenagers, most of them, who were not interested in excuses and used their fists freely. Jozef didn't want to be smacked about, so he checked the time once more.

It was quiet up on the hill, the only sound the whisper of the nighttime wind in the tall weeds. Here was where Jozef came to think about his former life, his wife and child, his apartment in Cracow, the office at the university where he'd prepared his lectures, and the coffee room down the hall. He'd liked to spend time there, gossiping with his fellow professors, avoiding university politics as much as possible, flirting with the secretaries.

All that was gone. He'd been separated from his family when, after being taken prisoner, they'd been put on different trains, sent to different camps. Were they alive or dead? He didn't know. The University of Cracow had been closed, his apartment in Cracow was now occupied by a German officer and his mistress. This might change, he knew, when the war ended, but for now, what he could do was fight back. So, as soon as he went to Kiel to work building the U-boats, he began hand-copying the workings of a torpedo detonator—then gave the schematic to a fellow prisoner who claimed to have a way of communicating with the Polish émigrés in Paris. They would know what to do with it—get it, somehow, to the British.

Looking down the hill, he saw another U-boat, which sounded its horn as it left port. He knew where it was going, up the canal, out into the Baltic. Then through the Skagerrak—an arm of the North Sea between Norway and Sweden— then out into the sea. The U-boat would then head up the west coast of Norway and turn northeast, where it would hunt the convoys of British freighters and the shipping of other nations as well, that brought arms, food, and oil to ports of Russia, to Murmansk and Archangel, making it possible for Russia to continue fighting the Germans.

Jozef watched as down below, on the canal, the U-boat continued its slow progress toward the Baltic. In the darkness, he could just make out a number painted near the top of the conning tower, but he couldn't read it. For that he would need some optical device. There was such a thing, he'd heard, special binoculars, large and ungainly, known as night glasses. If he'd had those, he thought, he could have truly spied on the U-boats, sending the identification, the number, the time, and the date, to the British, who tracked every ship in the Kriegsmarine. Putting such information into British hands would be difficult and dangerous, he knew, but he could, if he had the night glasses, make war on his captors.

It began to rain, just a light rain that pattered down on the hillside, and now it really was time to leave his refuge, so, very reluctantly, he walked slowly down the hill toward the abandoned school where the Poles now lived.

Ricard and Kasia walked along the wharf, trying to decide which bar had a room it rented out. To the east, they could see a mowed strip of land that led to a chain-link fence with barbed wire woven through it, then, above the chain link, three separate strands of wire. On the fence, a weathered sign: a red skull-and-crossbones next to the word ACHTUNG! Below it, a warning: PASSAGE BEYOND THIS POINT IS FORBIDDEN ON PAIN OF DEATH. Beyond the wire, a high brick wall. "That's the naval base," Ricard said.

Finally, in the middle of the wharf, they chose a bar with a carefully hand-painted sign: a bearded sailor peering through a telescope. They started to show their papers to the barman, but he waved them off. "You have a bed for us?" Ricard said.

"Jah, there's a room on the second floor, ten reichsmarks for the night."

As Ricard paid, a black Opel pulled up to the door, paused, then crossed the wharf and parked, but the driver remained in the car. Ricard didn't think much of it, he was very tired and he wanted to sleep. "Is there anything to eat?" Kasia asked the barman.

"I can get you some cheese and bread and a bottle of beer."

"We'll take it up to the room with us," Kasia said.

Kasia liked to walk around while she ate. Using a knife that had been included with their meal, Kasia cut off a piece of the orange cheese, then slid it off the blade and, as she began chewing, she wandered idly over to the window and stared out at the car as she ate. She cut a piece of the dense black bread, handed it to Ricard, and said, "Who is that out there, do you suppose?"

Ricard stood by her side at the window. "No idea. To do with us?"

Kasia shrugged.

Then the Opel's driver-side window was rolled down, and the young man with the reddish hair seemed to be looking directly at them. "Oh, it's him," Ricard said. "Maybe it's time to get out of here."

Together, they left the room and hurried downstairs to the bar—tired workers drinking beer—and took the back door, which opened on an alley with puddles of black water and fragrant garbage cans. From under a stairway, a cat scampered away.

"Where to hide?" Kasia said.

"Did you see a sign on the ferry dock that said SWEDEN?" Ricard said.

"Yes, there's a ferry waiting at the dock," Kasia said. "But maybe it's going to Denmark. **Occupied** Denmark."

"We'll have to take our chances," Ricard said. "Anywhere but here, as the saying goes." From an open space between buildings, they could see the small ferry, an ancient tub from a Popeye cartoon, puffs of black smoke rising from its crooked smokestack.

Now the driver of the Opel signaled to a stevedore occupied with coiling a tarred rope. The man came to the driver's window and the driver showed him a sheet of paper. "Bet you ten francs that's a wanted poster with a photograph," Kasia said. "Guess who."

"Merde," Ricard said.

"Merde, indeed," Kasia said. "We've got the fucking Gestapo after us. They've always got photographs."

"We'll have to cross the wharf to get to the ferry," Ricard said.

They left the alley and headed toward the ferry dock. From the Opel, two little taps on the horn, beep-beep. When they turned to look at the car, the driver crooked a finger and beckoned to them. "Time to leave," Ricard said. They walked faster, taking an angle which would lead them behind the trunk of the car. The driver waited, then, playing with them, began to back up very slowly. The two walked away from the car; the Opel followed. Passing a freighter, moored to the dock, Ricard saw a toolbox with an open lid, apparently belonging to a workman serving one of the winches. From a heap of tools in the box, Ricard took a shiny steel pliers. "Go talk to him," Ricard said. "Then wave me over."

Kasia went to the driver's window and the man with the reddish hair turned toward her. "What do you want with us?" she said.

The man opened his jacket to show Kasia an automatic in a shoulder holster. "Get in the car," he said. "Don't make me shoot you, we need to have a conversation."

"In the car . . . both of us?"

"Yes."

"Alright, I'll get my friend," she said and signaled to Ricard, who walked quickly, pretending to be worried and scared, over to the car. To see directly inside the car he had to bend his knees. Momentarily, the man's face relaxed—these people were going to obey him. Then Ricard hit him between the eyes with the pliers. Hit him harder than he'd intended, and the man's eyes rolled up and he collapsed sideways, draped across the front seat, out cold. Kasia rolled up the window and locked the door. Ricard followed her example on the other side of the Opel.

As they boarded the ferry to Sweden, there

was a crowd at the bow railing, waving goodby to friends, calling out "Wiedersehen! Wiedersehen!" and last-minute messages. Meanwhile, Ricard and Kasia watched the Opel. "What if he comes to?" Kasia said.

"He'll come staggering out of the car, calling for the police, and we shall be arrested. But, if he remains undiscovered, and the captain of this ship ever decides to sail, we will be leaving Germany, and I doubt we will return. Anyhow, cross your fingers, I hit him pretty hard."

Out on the wharf, some passersby did notice the car, a few of them peered inside, tapped on the window, then walked away. One man grabbed the door handle and yanked hard, but the lock held, while the next volunteer turned to his friend and made the classic gesture: fist with thumb extended, hand tilted above the mouth—**he's drunk.** He was followed by a policeman on a bicycle, who stopped to examine the situation, tried both doors, then shrugged and rode away. One big, brawny stevedore spent quite a while with the Opel—finally yelled "Everything alright?" and returned to work.

A few minutes later, as Ricard breathed a sigh of relief, the ferry sailed.

LEILA

AT LAST, BACK IN PARIS. RICARD UNLOCKED THE door to his apartment to find a thick sunbeam, with dust motes drifting through it, shining in the window. By the typewriter on his desk, a stack of paper titled **The Investigator.** He read part of a page, then part of another, saw something that had to be changed, reached for a pencil, and crossed out a word.

Then he opened the window and the street life of the city flowed in: barking dogs, mothers yelling out the window at their kids, the itinerant scissors sharpener calling out for customers, and that certain, very particular scent the city wore, compounded of age and dust and sewers and perfume and Gauloises smoke and potatoes frying in oil. Ricard inhaled deeply and knew he was home. He sprawled out on his bed, closed his eyes, and let the return to Paris gather in his heart.

But not for long. When he thought of what he had to do that evening, his spirits sank a little. Anne Legros, the editor at Éditions Montrésor he liked, was leaving Paris. He looked at his watch and saw that it was almost four o'clock, when the shops would reopen after the midday closure. He looped and knotted a gray wool scarf around his neck, tucked the ends inside his corduroy jacket, put on a pair of gloves, found the ration-stamp book in his desk drawer, took the string bag that hung on the doorknob, and headed out. There was an open-air market at the nearby Place Maubert, but it was the wrong day for that, so he would take the Pont Marie across the Seine, then head for the Rue Saint-Antoine, his favorite shopping street. He paused for a time midway across the Pont Marie and stared down at the heavy current in the Seine, the water gray beneath a gray November sky. His reverie was interrupted by a German patrol boat, cruising up the river. **Fucking war,** he thought, **you can't escape it.**

On the Rue Saint-Antoine, he stopped at the **crèmerie,** where the owner offered him a wedge of mimolette, a hard, orange cheese, from under the counter. Expensive, she told him, but ripe for supper tonight. He bought the mimolette. Next, he visited the butcher and bought a short length of sausage, then stopped at the **boulangerie** for a wedge of **pain de campagne,** a bread that would last forever. For his final stop, he went to a wine-shop and bought a bottle of red wine, the best he could afford.

Then he returned to the Rue de la Huchette and, with newspaper and twine, made a secure bundle of his purchases.

It was close to six, and dark, by the time he reached the building in the Sixth Arrondissement where Anne Legros lived. He'd called and she was waiting for him in front of her building.

"So," he said after greeting her, "you're on your way south."

"Yes, to my aunt's house in Lacaune."

As they walked to the Métro that would take them to the Gare de Lyon, he said, "What's it like there, in Lacaune?"

"Just the usual **petit village,** everybody knows everybody else. Very quiet, very **peaceful.** No Boche to be seen, so no controls, no demands for papers. My aunt has the **tabac** in the village, and I will work there and live in the big, old house she has at the edge of town."

"So then, no more Éditions Montrésor. I am sure they're sorry to see you go."

"They are, but I can't stay in Paris any longer. With all the Germans and the Gestapo, I began to get a bad feeling, as though something awful was going to happen. When I saw people taken away in the Gestapo vans, I thought, someday that will be me. So, farewell to Paris, as much as I love it. But you will stay?"

"As long as I can," Ricard said. "I was born here, I belong to the city."

They rode the Métro to the Gare de Lyon and fought their way through the crowd to the train for Orléans, the first leg of Madame Legros's voyage to the south, then walked along the platform, to a coach that wasn't yet jammed with passengers.

"I'm sorry to see you go," Ricard said.

"I'm sorry to leave, but it's for the best."

Ricard handed her the newspaper parcel of food and said, "You'll be on the trains for a day or two, so I brought you something to eat."

"Thank you, Ricard," she said. "You are a good soul."

They embraced. Madame Legros climbed the first step to the train, turned, and waved, and then she was gone.

It was early December, a dusting of new snow on the ground, the Schönbrun-Grandschule high school where the Poles lived stood isolated and dark in what had once been a village adjacent to the city of Kiel. Not much left of the village now; the RAF bombers came in 1940. The school stood among a few remnants of brick wall with weeds growing where a building had stood. The school itself had been built in the middle of the nineteenth century, with SCHÖNBRUN-GRANDSCHULE chiseled into the elaborate stonework below the roof. The teachers of those days had likely been a formidable group, bearded men who wore pince-nez and stiff collars, droning away in their classrooms as the students sat at attention.

Abandoned in 1910, the school had been reopened as a barracks for the Polish laborers sent to Germany to build submarines: thirty cots spread among the classrooms, old WCs brought back to working order. On that night in early December, Jozef and three other workers waited for their Ukrainian guards to go to sleep, then held a meeting and talked about resistance.

How to fight back against the Germans? Soon the conversation centered on their work on the torpedo detonators they built for the Germans. "Why not," one of them suggested, "build an extra one and hand it over to the British?"

The detonator was eight inches in height, its exterior surface made of highly polished chrome steel. The front end, the top, was curved, while the flat bottom had four holes bored in it where electrical cables would be plugged in when the torpedo was put together. The device was sensitive to contact, or to depth and distance, and, once it reached a ship it would set off the explosive in the torpedo, blowing a ten-foot hole in the hull and sending the ship to the bottom.

The Polish workers would have to fabricate this device for every torpedo they constructed, and, aware that it was important to the German war effort, they had decided to build one for the British. This was espionage, and could get them arrested and tortured, but they didn't care. They were **Poles**, Polish patriots, so they fought their enemies.

To get the device to the British secret service, they would have to take it to Paris, and for this job, they chose as courier one of their number called Ostrow.

His documents for the trip were created by substituting his name and description on papers belonging to one of the other workers, the money for his journey stolen from shops in the city of Kiel. A few years earlier, before the attack on Poland in 1939, Ostrow had worked as a welder in the shipyards of Gdynia, on Poland's Baltic coast. Then he'd been captured during the invasion of Poland and, having a trade the Germans needed, was spared prison camp and sent to the naval shipyards in Kiel.

On the train from Hamburg to Paris—by way of changes in Emden and Brussels—Ostrow stood in the packed aisle, hand tight on his small valise. It was the common version of a valise: tan, pliable canvas with handle and buckled straps made of cheap leather. What made it unusual was that it held a detonator, wrapped in well-used underwear to discourage customs officers. Ostrow himself would be of little interest to the officers; he looked like a typical worker, a short man who wore an oil-stained cap with tufts of gray hair sticking out above his ears, an old blue winter jacket, and oil-stained shoes with newspaper stuffed inside because the soles were tearing away and his feet were cold.

Then, at the customs inspection on the German side of Emden, his luck ran out. The German inspector was fifty-two. He'd begun his job at the age of twenty-three. He'd seen everything, so he knew, instinctively, when a traveler had contraband—morphine, weapons, stolen gems, he'd seen it all. But what annoyed the inspector most of all was that he was now facing a Pole, a "subhuman," according to Nazi doctrine.

"Open your valise." The inspector used the eraser end of a pencil to probe through the clothes in Ostrow's valise. He turned up the underwear-wrapped detonator, told Ostrow to unwrap it, then said, "What's this?" Ostrow had been well coached by the other Poles at Kiel, and the question wasn't unexpected. "An oil pump for a sports car," he said. "It's for a friend of mine in Paris, he's got some fancy Italian automobile, it can go a hundred and fifty miles an hour." The inspector wasn't sure about it, and did what, in such cases, he'd been told to do: he met the eyes of one of the Gestapo men observing the line. The officer was young and wore a blue suit, with his hair combed up in a pompadour. This man confirmed the inspector's gesture, waited as Ostrow had his exit visa stamped, then followed him as he left the office and stood waiting on the platform for the train to Brussels. Here Ostrow found himself standing next to a middle-aged woman with a leather case. "Cold, today," Ostrow said, rubbing his hands. The woman looked him over and decided he wasn't someone she would answer. The man in the blue suit signaled to a colleague and nodded at the woman—**Find out who she is.**

The man in the blue suit's colleague, a Gestapo officer wearing a leather jacket, approached the woman, showed a badge, and wrote down her name, address, and passport number.

The train for Brussels pulled in a few minutes later. It was already crowded, and Ostrow had to push his way past passengers riding on the iron steps that led to the carriage vestibule. "Excuse me," he said, polite words accompanying very impolite pushes and shoves. The passengers inside were as usual: war-weary, unsmiling, stiff and cold after hours of standing on the train, muttering under their breath as Ostrow forced his way among them. Life was easier for the men following him: they showed badges, and people squeezed themselves out of their way. Finally, a conductor, using both hands and a shoe, forced travelers on the steps up into the crowded vestibule and signaled to the engineer.

Slowly, the overloaded train began to move. It rattled past harvested fields, where gray light reflected off pools of standing water under a low, dark sky, past long stretches of winter weeds bending in the wind, past forests of trees with bare branches, past the empty streets of the occasional village.

On the train, the passengers stared out at the flat, featureless landscape. They were a hundred and eighty miles from Paris, six hours on the slow train. But it took longer. Just after entering Holland, the train reached a section of track that had been blown up—by RAF bombers or Resistance saboteurs— and here the train was led by a railwayman who walked ahead of the locomotive and waved it forward over track that had been newly laid. The train crept along, bumping over temporary connections installed by railway crews. The passengers were silent, keeping their opinions of bombers and saboteurs to themselves. It was nine in the evening before the train arrived at the Gare du Nord and the passengers were at last released from captivity.

Kasia and Ricard were waiting for Ostrow on the platform. They'd had a letter describing him, "My uncle will arrive . . . ," and they knew what he looked like. They watched him leave the train, and they saw the two officers following him. Who were these travelers—solidly built and self-confident young fellows with no luggage and busy eyes? "He's being followed," Ricard said. "The guy in the blue suit? That's a Gestapo thug, I'd bet my life on it."

"I see him," Kasia said. "And the other one, in the leather jacket."

Ostrow peered down the platform. Jozef had described the young woman he was supposed to meet and, when he saw Kasia, he started to approach her. But she merely glanced at him, then looked away. Was he mistaken? Was there another attractive woman with short hair wearing a brown suit? Ostrow didn't see her. Now what? He waited while the arriving passengers met family or friends, waited while others headed for the taxi line outside the station. Meanwhile, the two Gestapo officers watched the platform and waited for Ostrow to meet somebody or head off into the city.

Kasia swore under her breath, she could see the valise, she knew what was inside, but to acknowledge Ostrow at this point was to be arrested. Still, they couldn't just leave him standing there, by now nearly alone as the other passengers dispersed. Finally, Ricard said, "We have to get that valise."

"How?" Kasia said.

"Let's steal it," Ricard said. "Such things happen around railway stations."

"What about the Gestapo escort?" Kasia said.

"We'll lose them. Go talk to him."

Kasia headed for Ostrow. When she reached him she said, "Welcome to Paris, monsieur. Are you seeking a taxi? My friend is waiting, just around the corner."

"What? A taxi? No, aren't you the woman I'm . . . ?"

Ricard came up on the other side of Ostrow, deftly removed the valise from his fingers, and hurried away toward the Boulevard de Magenta. Both Gestapo officers followed Ricard and the valise.

There were Parisian policemen here and there, but the German officers knew they couldn't depend on help from the French. They could have arrested Ostrow—as Gestapo men they could have arrested anyone they liked—but they wanted his contact—who would receive the valise?

Meanwhile, Ostrow started to run after Ricard, but Kasia grabbed him by the back of his coat. "Time for you to disappear," she said in Polish. Pressing a wad of francs into his hand, she said, "Here's money for your things." Then she ran and caught up with Ricard, who was in turn being trailed by the two officers.

By now, Ricard was walking fast and saw, in a café window, that his pursuers were closing in on him. "Now we split up," he said to Kasia. "Meet me back at the **gare.**" Kasia, a lot faster than Ricard, turned suddenly and ran across the street, but the Gestapo officers ignored her and followed Ricard and the valise.

Ricard now began to panic and broke into a run, but he was forty and they were in their twenties, and he wasn't going to outdistance them. He looked up the boulevard and spotted an approaching taxi, the usual wood-fired engine set atop its roof. The taxi slowed as it neared a sharp corner; Ricard pulled the door open and sprawled full-length across the backseat.

Or rather, across the laps of the two people sitting in the backseat: a glamorous woman in a hat with a veil, who yelped as Ricard landed on her, and an older man, a Parisian dandy, a gent, with a white mustache curled up at the ends, who wore a white suit over a waistcoat with fleur-de-lis designs on white silk. He had also an ornate walking stick with which he began to beat Ricard, shouting insults at him in upper-class French. The taxi jerked to a stop and the driver scurried to the backseat, grabbed Ricard by the shoulders, and attempted to pull him out, but Ricard swung the valise and smacked him full on the nose, which began to bleed copiously. From the older gent, the French equivalent of **Damn you, sir, have you no manners?**

Now a **flic** came running and blowing his whistle. Ricard didn't wait for more police to arrive; he slid the rest of the way out of the car, ran around to the driver's seat, and put the car in gear. The woman squawked, "Maurice! We are being kidnapped! Do something!" From behind, Maurice hit Ricard on the top of his head. Ricard saw stars, then stopped the taxi and punched the white-haired gent in the forehead. Shaking his hand, hurt by the impact, Ricard said, "I am with the Resistance. I'm being followed."

"Go resist somewhere else," the gent yelled and swung his stick back for another blow as, once again, a police whistle sounded. Ricard dragged him out of the taxi, set him on the pavement, put a foot behind his heel, and gave him a good shove. The man tumbled backward with a curse, Ricard jumped into the taxi and drove off. From the backseat, the gent's companion cried out, "Please, sir, let me go, I'll give you money."

Behind the taxi, a police car approached, its two-tone Klaxon horn honking away, and drew abreast of the taxi. From the passenger seat, the Gestapo man in the blue suit shook his fist at Ricard, who turned hard left and slammed the taxi into the police car. Both vehicles mounted the curb, the police car skidded to a stop in front of a building, the taxi hit a streetlamp, which broke the lamp from its standard and sent it crashing down on the taxi's roof. Ricard grabbed the valise and took off running down the boulevard.

Almost immediately he found himself by a department store and hurried inside. The perfume counter was near the entry and a saleswoman, speaking from a cloud of scent, said, "Monsieur, do you need help? You are injured." Ricard realized that his forehead was wet and drew a finger across it, which came away red. "I'm running from the Boche," he said to the woman, who made a sound of sympathy and began wiping Ricard's forehead with a facial tissue—then handed him another. "Take the elevator," she said. "We have five floors."

As Ricard waited by the elevator, he heard a commotion at the front of the store—the Gestapo had arrived. He watched the needle above the elevator door as it descended: fourth floor, third, second, and there it stopped. Behind him, he heard running footsteps. Then the needle began to descend, the door opened automatically, and the elevator operator, wearing white gloves, slid the gate aside. A small crowd entered the elevator and, just before the gate was closed, so did the Gestapo man in the leather jacket. The elevator car filled with shoppers, Ricard stood against the side of the car, with several people between him and the Gestapo officer. Ricard dabbed at his hairline with the tissue.

Then the man in the leather jacket spoke, his French bearing a heavy German accent. "Give up this foolishness," he said. "We just want to talk to you."

"Go fuck yourself," Ricard said.

"We mean you no harm, monsieur."

"Go back to Germany, you **grand cul.**"

"Just hand over the valise and I won't trouble you further."

"**Casse-toi.**" Piss off.

The elevator operator called out, "Second floor. Ladies' fashion." The door opened and he slid the gate aside. "Excuse me," Ricard said, and worked his way toward the door. As he stepped out, he heard the Gestapo man say, "Excuse me, I'm getting off here."

But he couldn't get off, the Parisian men and women in the elevator jostled him and pressed around him, all of them staring straight ahead and pretending that nothing was happening.

The Gestapo man swore in German; somebody on the elevator called him a dirty Boche. As the door closed, the officer struggled, but the crowd had him penned in, and now the elevator left. Ricard headed for the stairs, ran down to the first floor and out onto the boulevard. He took a moment to get his bearings, then headed for the Métro.

Ricard met with Leila at an empty apartment in the elegant La Muette district, the best neighborhood in the high-class Sixteenth Arrondissement. The tenants were away—maybe at their country houses, maybe in New York for the duration of the war. Meanwhile, the apartment had been carefully protected; the shutters were closed tight and every piece of furniture, sofas, chairs, tables, beds, even the dog's little bed, had been covered with sheets.

On a sheet-covered sofa, Leila sat with back ramrod straight, head high, thighs, knees, and feet pressed together. He found her, as before, intensely desirable: thick, black hair combed back on both sides, Mediterranean complexion, gently curved nose, and dark gray eyes. She had her coat over her arm and wore a tweed Chanel suit—hip-length jacket, knee-length skirt—a necklace of lustrous, silvery-white pearls, and carried a leather overnight bag. After brief small talk, she explained the site of their meeting by saying, "My friends are generous with their apartment keys."

"You have others you can use?"

"Oh yes. In my business, one must have safe houses."

"That would be the spying business?"

"That's what I do, Monsieur Ricard."

"For a long time?"

"Since I was sixteen." She smiled at the memory.

"How, um, did you come to . . . get into that business?"

"It runs in families, that's the secret, so one comes to it naturally. We are Turkish, my family is, but we operate wherever the political moment takes us. My uncle worked for the Greeks, and spied on the Turks, the Ottoman Turks, just before their empire collapsed, in 1918. Of course he was paid in gold, British gold sovereigns, one doesn't want to work for paper currency, not ever, though Swiss francs are sometimes acceptable. My great-aunt learned that the hard way, she spied for the Croats against the Serbs and had a hellish time of it, her safe-deposit box stuffed with Croatian kuna, which she had to convert to gold jewelry. We go back a long way, Monsieur Ricard, some of the family say the Renaissance, but who knows. I lost two ancestors who worked against the Russians in 1903—the Okhrana secret police made them disappear, and ever since we've demanded a high price to operate against Russia."

"And now, you work for the British."

Leila nodded. "This is a big war, we have now, and we've had all sorts of offers, but we chose with our hearts, and it wasn't hard to choose. We certainly wanted no part of the Nazis. We don't work for monsters."

Ricard unbuckled the valise and brought out the detonator. "This took some doing, but here it is."

Leila leaned forward on the sheet-covered sofa and Ricard handed her the device. As she held it in her slim hands, nails polished in carmine red, Ricard was struck by the incongruity. "It seems plain enough," she said. "But I suppose what makes it interesting is whatever goes on under the covering. Let's have a look inside."

Ricard was horrified and his face showed it.

"Now, now, Ricard, I'm just teasing you." After a moment she looked at him inquisitively and said, "Of course there will be more from your Polish friends."

Ricard shrugged and said, "I don't know, the people who brought it here did it on their own."

"Do you pay them?"

"No."

"Better if you did. Clearer. We respect the impulse for resistance, we depend on it, but you may say of us, 'They have plenty of money, why not make your life better?'"

"What will you do with it?"

"Make sure it gets to the proper people, in London, the people who run these things and have all the strings in their hands. And, I promise you, they will want more. They'll put it in an amiable way—they are forever polite—but they'll ask." Leila opened her overnight bag and put the device away. She paused a moment, met Ricard's eyes, then stood up. "I must be going," she said, reached into her purse and produced a thick wad of occupation francs. "Here's something for you—you can pay people whatever they need or use it yourself." She handed Ricard a form; his name had been typed across the top line. "And you have to sign for it. Have you a pen?"

Ricard took out his pen and signed the document. It was then that he realized he was caught, that he would work for Leila as long as the war went on—in one way an uninviting prospect. He knew that he and Kasia had been lucky, they hadn't been caught. But, next time? At least he would remain close to Leila.

She was mysterious, remote, unapproachable, and she fascinated him—he had never known a woman remotely like her. So, in the way of the world, that made her intensely desirable. Of course, he, a mere writer, would **never** remove that stylish suit and what she wore beneath it. Lacy underwear? White cotton panties? Still, though a mere writer, he had a good imagination, with which he undressed her, and was delighted, and inflamed, by what he discovered.

Leila returned to her apartment in the Chaussée de la Muette, then walked over to a deluxe gift shop which carried **objets: bijoux fantaisie**— costume jewelry—and small statuettes, in onyx or crystal, meant for those with money to spend on lovers or friends. The proprietor, whom she'd known and trusted for a long time, led her to a room behind the office. With so many lovely things to buy in Paris, gift wrapping had become a specialty of the city's better shops. Very much the maestro, the proprietor wrapped the detonator in crinkly white paper, set it in a gold gift box with mauve paper, and tied it with a purple ribbon. Leila stepped back to admire the creation—very fancy, she thought. And very safe.

Given the way that Leila dressed and held herself, and the impressive presentation of the package, she knew that the customs officers at Orly airfield would not ask that it be unwrapped. This was not the first time she had disguised contraband objects, and she knew it would work.

At Orly airfield, Leila found her pilot friend and gave him an envelope—he was always pleased to see her. An hour later, she boarded a Potez 56, a low-wing monoplane built of plywood, which flew the mail from Paris to Madrid, a seven-hour trip with a refueling stop at Rivesaltes airfield in Perpignan. The wind was blowing hard that morning, with streaks of gray cloud moving overhead, and the plane shuddered and plunged as the pilot, seated directly in front of Leila, fought with the controls and talked to himself in a language she didn't recognize. There was one other seat on the Potez—the rest of the plane was packed with canvas mailbags—and it was occupied, just before takeoff, by a military officer of some nation, who didn't fly well, and, for the entire trip, hugged a briefcase to his chest with both arms, all the while praying, or cursing, under his breath.

In Madrid, Leila called an accommodation number, a Thomas Cook travel agency, and told them she would be at the Hôtel Miramar, old, rundown, twelve rooms. There, Leila took a room and waited for a telephone call. Twenty minutes later, the phone croaked and, on the other end, an Englishman speaking Spanish told her to go to the Restaurante Sobrino de Botín. She took a taxi there and waited at the reception desk.

She didn't wait long. Two civil servants from the British embassy, the second secretary and the political officer, joined her and they sat down to eat lunch. The Sobrino de Botín was said to be the world's oldest restaurant—opened in 1725. The long, narrow room, built of stone, was barrel-vaulted, the ceiling arching overhead. When their sherries arrived, Leila presented her gift-wrapped package, and the civil servants, who did espionage duty at the embassy, took turns in the WC, inspecting the gift, and returned to the table with grateful smiles.

They ordered the specialty, **sopa de ajo,** an egg poached in chicken broth flavored with garlic and sherry, and asked Leila, in their smooth, tenor voices, when she would have more presents for them. Not if, when. It was 1942, Britain was not winning the war, but they were no longer losing, and the time had come to go on the offensive.

They had, first of all, to win the war of blockades. In October of 1942, fifty-six merchant ships had been put out of commission, which meant that food, war matériel, and, crucially, oil, did not reach the United Kingdom. Thus RAF bombers hit the naval yards in Kiel for three nights, destroying the U-boat pens, the cranes, and the workshops, and flattening the Schönbrun-Grandschule lycée where the Polish laborers were housed. The Poles themselves were lucky; at work in an underground factory when the bombs fell. For the German engineers, there was no point in trying to rebuild, so they shifted the U-boat manufacture west, to France, to existing naval yards at the port of

Saint-Nazaire—closer to the RAF bombers but heavily protected by anti-aircraft emplacements and Luftwaffe fighter planes.

Meanwhile, Paul Ricard was at work in his garret, adding slow pages to **The Investigator,** hoping that Julien Montrésor, his publisher, was busy with other projects. Each time the telephone rang, he hesitated to answer it, afraid that Montrésor was going to hound him. But the publisher did not call.

Who did call was Leila. She wanted to meet with him, and had chosen for the meeting a room at the Grand Hôtel, in the Opéra district. Waiting for him in the lobby, she led him upstairs to a handsomely furnished room on the top floor.

It was five-thirty in the afternoon, the lights in the room were low, Leila was wearing a black silk dress, tied at the waist with the same material, a soft, supple, revealing dress. "Shall we have drinks sent up?" she said. "A brandy? A glass of wine?"

"No, not tonight, let's have whiskey sodas, tonight."

The telephone was on a nightstand by the bed and he watched, avidly, the shifting black silk as she walked over to call room service. After calling, she stood at the window for a moment, then said, "Strange, a dark city, I'll never get used to it." He joined her at the window, their shoulders almost touching, then, magically, touching. On the street below them, Parisians were going home from work, bundled up against the icy wind, walking quickly with heads down to spare their faces from the cold. "The world goes on," she said, taking his hand. "Sometimes I would like to live a different life, an everyday life."

"You would be bored soon enough," Ricard said. "You require excitement, I think."

"Yes, I suppose you're right. Still . . ." When there was a tap at the door, she said, "Our drinks."

Ricard went to get them. In the hall, a bellboy wearing a rakishly tilted cap held a silver tray with the drinks, the soda water bubbling in tall glasses. Ricard tipped him, then set the tray on a low table in front of a sofa. Leila sat down and patted the cushion next to her. "Don't be a stranger," she said, smiling at him.

"Salut," Ricard said. They clinked glasses and sipped at the whiskey soda.

"Well, I felt that," she said.

Ricard said, "Me too."

"We can do better," she said. Opening her purse, she took out a small glass jar that had once held caviar, and a tiny silver spoon. In the jar, white powder. She filled the spoon and held it up to his nose. He sniffed it up, she then helped herself. "Again?" she said.

"Why not?"

"You like cocaine?"

He nodded, face numb, then drank some whiskey soda.

She lit a cigarette and, eyes closed, exhaled

plumes of smoke from her nose, closed her eyes, and rested her head on the sofa. Then she looked at him and said, "Feeling good?"

"Better than good."

He was silent for a time, glad, more than glad, for her gracious presence. She came from a different world, richer than his, a world of aristocrats. But now, in this hotel room in Paris, they were about to make love, to be no more than two lovers with the long night to themselves.

"Why don't you take off your dress?" he said.

She laughed and stood up. "Glad you said that. I was going to spill my drink on it, accidentally on purpose." She untied the belt, then took the dress by the hem, wriggled out of it, and tossed it over the back of a chair. She was wearing snug white cotton panties, cut low on top and high on the bottom. When she unclipped her garters and rolled her stockings off, he saw that her legs were smooth and white. He stroked them and said, "Sit on my lap?" She made herself comfortable, then leaned forward a little and kissed him briefly on the forehead, took her panties off, and said, "Get undressed, Ricard, and, while you're at it, can we have music?"

He did as she asked, wobbling a little when he stood, then he walked over to a radio on the night table. She watched every step, enjoying the show. Ricard turned the radio on and worked the needle around the dial, passing a serious conversation— German political propaganda—a comedian with a laughing audience, brassy circus music, a heavy symphony, then, at last, Glenn Miller, "Moonlight Serenade."

He returned to the sofa, she sat again on his lap and nestled close to him, her arm around his neck. "Look what I found," she said, her hand between his legs.

Ricard stroked her as before, then moved his hand beneath her—she was very warm there. Gently at first, and slowly, he began to move his fingers back and forth. Then faster, pressing harder, encouraged by the change in her breathing. At last she made a quiet sound, an **oh,** closed her eyes, swayed, and fell back against him.

After a moment she said, "Let's turn off the lights."

He turned off the lights and they lay facing each other on the couch. A few minutes later, he thought she might be asleep, but she wasn't. Ricard lit a cigarette and, by the flare of the match, saw that she was staring at him, the look in her eyes tender, warm, and radiant. **Love in time of war,** he thought.

In the morning, heavy cloud overhead as fog settled on the city and softened the outlines of the buildings. Ricard liked fog, he used it in his books and enjoyed it in person, the real Paris made into a real noir film, and, somehow, it shrouded the noise of the city. Ricard, feeling the effects of the cocaine and the whiskey, had to peer through the gloom, using street signs to find his way home. He thought about Leila as he walked, about certain moments, about what they might do the next time they were together. When he was a few steps away from the Rue de la Huchette, he saw a Renault automobile parked in front of a café. He had to squint to see the driver. It was Teodor, the British agent.

Teodor said, "The civil servants in London want you to go to Saint-Nazaire, where the Germans have occupied the submarine base. The London message was urgent, because British and Allied shipping is being destroyed from there. Now the London people have bought a café in Saint-Nazaire, so you'll have cover for operations there. The café is called Le Relais, and you will act as owner and manager."

"What about Kasia?"

"She'll stay in Paris. They want her to do other things."

"When do I go?"

"Today or tomorrow."

"Then I'd better go home and pack my valise."

Saint-Nazaire. The heart of the beast.

Ricard had been there before and found it a busy, commercial port. The town was located at the southern end of Brittany, near the town of Nantes, where the river Loire emptied into the Atlantic. Once upon a time, the port had been a sleepy Breton fishing village. In 1914 it grew into a town known for its dry docks and shipbuilding industry and its **maisons tolérées**—its brothels. Now it was a war city. Walking from the railway station to the Place Marceau, site of the Café Le Relais, Ricard passed naval guard-posts where, twice, he had to produce his papers. The Germans were taking no chances here because this was the front line of the U-boat war: anti-aircraft positions every other block, their crews lounging on the emplacements, sitting on purloined garden chairs, smoking, sunning themselves, waiting for the next RAF attack.

It would come. For every submarine damaged, more than a few merchant ships survived.

On a street that faced the waterfront, Ricard saw a beached U-boat, its superstructure bent and twisted by gunfire, where wounded sailors, in Kriegsmarine uniforms, were being carried off the boat on stretchers. Many buildings had been hit by RAF bombs, façades tumbled into the street, revealing piles of wreckage, mounds of burnt brick and broken glass. The Germans clearly could not protect the town.

What they could protect, Ricard saw, were the U-boats themselves, which were berthed in a line of pens beneath a concrete roof thirty feet thick.

In time, he reached the Place Marceau, a block

from the waterfront, and there found the Café Le Relais. The interior was dark, a hand-lettered sign on the door said FERMÉ. Not far from the **place,** he found the office of the notary, its windows boarded up, where he retrieved the keys to the café and the names of its three former employees; the barman Louis, the waitress Marcelle, and Victorine—Vicki, the cook. He found two of them right away, left a note for the third, and they showed up the following day, ready to put the café back in order.

Louis the barman was short, with slicked-back hair, and talkative, rattling on endlessly about nothing in particular, a barman's stock-in-trade. **Never** politics; bad manners in France to raise such issues. Instead, observations on life in general, customers always had something to say about that: marriage, family, work. And Louis—who preferred his name said in the English manner, **Louie**—had a real gift for chatter about the weather. He'd lived his whole life in Saint-Nazaire and he knew when a storm was coming, or when they needed rain, or how long the humidity would stick around. A true prophet of the weather, Louie the barman.

Marcelle the waitress was fiftyish and seductively plump, well worth ogling in her snug waitress uniform—black dress and white apron—and Ricard ogled her attentively as she washed down the twelve tables in the café, Ricard daydreaming about finding themselves alone after work. As for Vicki the cook, she was seventy, white-haired and foulmouthed. "Ahh, fuck this fucking thing," she would say of her whisk. Vicki had always a cigarette dangling from her lips, she never flicked it, simply let the ash fall into the omelet or the **soupe de légumes.**

Ricard, suddenly the manager of a café, planned to work behind the bar. He learned to operate the glass-washing device, a grille with a spout below it that shot a spurt of cold water into the upside-down glass. That was it, no soap, no sponge, just one squirt and, after a swipe with a bar towel, the glass was ready for the next customer.

As for the food and drink supply, Ricard was that day visited by a short, squat fellow in a chalk-stripe, double-breasted suit, his provisioner, known as Pinky. Pinky laid it out for him: "We always have fish, you buy it on the dock when the fishing boats come in at night. There's some mackerel and sea bass, but mostly you'll get cod, everybody in Saint-Nazaire eats codfish, we're raised on it. But, if you want to serve more than cod, you'll have to buy from the farmers. Maybe once a week a scrawny old chicken for the soup, they grow lentils and **haricots,** beans, white and black. There's a farmer a few miles from town who owns a milk cow and once a week he sells cheese, hard, yellow cheese. I don't think it has a name, we just call it cheese."

Pinky paused a moment, then said, "As for the wine and the beer, that you'll buy from me. Early in the occupation, the Germans took all the wine back to Germany, or at least they think they did. Let's say they took bottles with fancy labels, Château this and Château that, but the wine itself isn't what the label says it is, it's Château Made-Last-Week. The vintners are some of the craftiest people in this country and that's saying something. If you want the real thing you have to go down to the wineries and buy it in plain bottles. As for the beer, it's the same story: the old names, alright, but made right here in Saint-Nazaire where the labels are printed."

Ricard, behind the bar, searched the shelves below the bar, and poured out a Hennessy cognac. Pinky drained the tiny glass and smacked his lips. "Thank you, my friend," he said, and Ricard poured him another.

So, for a time, it went. Louie poured the drinks and gossiped with the customers, Vicki cooked the food and Marcelle served it. The winter waned in February, a few nice days, warm sun and blue skies, as a tease, then back to chill winds and darkness at four in the afternoon. March came in like a lion and went out like a lion, the patrons had to pull hard on the café door because the wind wanted it open. There followed the rains of April—that year a month true to its songs. But the rain didn't beat down as it had in winter, there were days when it could have been May, and people left their umbrellas home. Every morning, Ricard looked out at the sea, calmer now, and felt that his life was improving with the season. Marcelle knew he liked her and encouraged his interest, her body touching his, as though by accident, as they went about the daily chores of running a café.

Once they opened, Ricard found that the café was being used as a clandestine letter box. People stopped by and left messages, which were then picked up the next hour, or the next day. It wasn't a hard job, but Ricard knew it could be dangerous—a prize for the Gestapo, who could have followed the visitors, or arrested them then and there. And likely Ricard as well.

Meanwhile, the U-boats returned home from hunting, or sometimes didn't. The RAF bombed the city now and again, windows were boarded up— no glass—and funerals were held. There had been a serious raid in March, the submarine pens and docks damaged. Repairs were made and the battle at sea continued. According to the BBC, the Wehrmacht was advancing toward the city of Stalingrad but was periodically pushed back and had to fight once more to regain lost territory.

Then, one afternoon in April, Teodor left a note at the café and Ricard met him at an open-air fish market. "One of the Polish resistance groups in London," Teodor said, "is planning to run an operation here in Saint-Nazaire, and they want you to work with them."

"Who are they?"

"They're the resistance movement of the Polish

upper class, known as the Cichociemni, the Silent and Unseen. They've been operating against the Germans since 1941."

A woman wearing a rubber apron emptied a bucket of ice on a zinc-covered stand stocked with herrings, and the two men moved away from her. "When do I meet them?" Ricard said.

"There's a representative here, back in the office."

Teodor walked Ricard down an aisle that led to the office, then disappeared. In the office, the Polish representative was leaning on the edge of a desk, drinking a cup of coffee. The man greeted him as "Monsieur Ricard," then said, "Sometimes I use the name Erik." He'd been born and raised in Poland, he told Ricard, but had been living in Paris since the midthirties. He was clearly an upper-class gentleman, tall and thin, once an athlete, someone who could have lived a life of leisure if he'd wanted to, but the attack on Poland had led him, and some of his friends, to form a resistance organization. His French was fluent and sophisticated, his clothing expensive and casual: blazer jacket, open-collared shirt, and a diamond-pattern slipover sweater.

"Have you been in Saint-Nazaire a long time?" he asked.

"Three months, I'm running a café. Not a bad job. People, all sorts, all day and night. Where do you live, in Paris?"

"Here and there," Erik said, with a smile both friendly and deflective. "For the time being. Paris is the heart of the world, to me, but until the war is over I can't settle down. You know the law of the fugitive: don't sleep in the same place for more than one night. Well, I don't quite do that, but, truth is, I don't stay anywhere for long. I'm forever a stranger, but that's how it is when you do clandestine work."

Looking over Erik's shoulder, Ricard watched a U-boat leaving the dock. Erik turned to see what had caught his attention and said, "There goes a Type IX submarine, the Germans' top-line U-boat. It has all the latest technology, but it needs a lot of sailors to operate—a crew of forty-eight, all volunteers."

"Not for me," Ricard said. "The idea of being underwater . . ."

For this operation, Ricard brought Kasia from Paris. Her job was to watch the German barracks and memorize the schedule kept by the sailors as they were brought by bus to the U-boats at the dock. The buses were painted naval gray and had wire mesh that protected the windows from hand grenades. Kasia, to blend in with the local population, wore a gray shawl over her head and an old overcoat.

Still, she was noticed. On the afternoon of her second day at this job she was confronted by a German guard, a classic Prussian type with a lavish mustache, groomed to a point at each end. He came up behind Kasia, put a hand on her shoulder, and turned her around. "Your papers, Fräulein," he said, very stern and official.

Kasia produced her papers, the policeman looked at them, and said, "What are you doing in Saint-Nazaire? These papers allow you to live in Paris."

Kasia was startled, put a hand to her heart, and said, "You frightened me, Officer."

"I'm waiting for your answer. You've been around here since yesterday."

Kasia nodded, tears starting in her eyes. "I am waiting to see my . . . friend."

"Are you. And does your friend have a name?"

"He is called Franz, Officer. Franz Miller." Now two tears rolled down Kasia's cheeks.

"And Franz is in the navy?"

"That's what he told me."

"And he is, I would guess, a very **good** friend, a very **close** friend."

Kasia said, anguish in her voice, "I just wanted to see him, to talk to him."

"Because you are in love with him?"

"Because I am pregnant."

The old-fashioned Prussian shook his head, **too much sin in the world now.** "I can do one of two things with you, young lady. I'm sorry for your predicament, but you can't linger at military instal-lations. So I will have to take you to the police station, or you can be on your way. Someday you'll see Franz again, but not now. Which shall it be?"

Kasia took a handkerchief from her pocket and wiped away her tears. "I will go away from here," she said.

The policeman patted her shoulder and said, "There, there, it will all come right in the end."

Ricard and Kasia rented a room in Saint-Nazaire to use as a base of operation, made contact with Jacquot—Kasia's gangster friend—at a seaside bar, and the three had dinner at the hotel, then waited until ten in the evening to enter the port office. It was Erik who had ordered the intrusion, needing a way to surveil the port. In front of the two-story building, a sailor wearing a holstered sidearm guarded the front door. Quietly, Jacquot led them around to the alley that ran behind the building. At the back door, no guard. Jacquot took a metal key used to open a sardine tin and carefully jimmied the lock open. Then, using a flashlight, they entered the port office.

On the ground floor, a directory showed the office of the port captain to be in room 27 on the second floor. The office was unlocked and the three entered, then Ricard rummaged through the files to find what he wanted: an entry permit, and a refitting order, in this case for U-boat 521, the **Freya**. Ricard took that, and a few other papers that he thought Erik might use later.

They left through the back door—Jacquot had made sure it could be relocked—and walked through the warm night back to the hotel, where Ricard paid Jacquot two hundred American dollars. In the hotel room, Ricard shared the bed with Kasia. Restless, Ricard left Kasia sleeping and looked out the window. A bus, painted gray with grilled windows, moved slowly up the street, taking a crew to their U-boat for a nighttime departure.

The following day, Ricard and Kasia took the train back to Paris, while Jacquot went off on his own. Kasia returned to her room near the stockyards, Ricard went back to his garret on the Rue de la Huchette. The lights on the dock came on at seven P.M., then, that night, the RAF, in wave after wave of bombers, badly damaged the port of Saint-Nazaire. The BBC reported it, the Parisians talked about it, and the general feeling was that it would take some time to rebuild.

The civil servants held a meeting in April.

Not in London, where the German bombing had changed the city—gentlemen could no longer go to their clubs, because their clubs had been turned to rubble, along with the streets where they'd stood.

So they met at one of their number's country houses, in Sussex, and made several decisions. They would continue to use Ricard as their operative in occupied France. He would work for Leila, and also for a man called Adrian, a dependable veteran spy who would approach Ricard as soon as possible.

The most important task for Ricard would be the theft of one of the new German torpedoes. The British had the detonator, thanks to Ricard and his friend Kasia, and now, at the urgent demands of the defense ministries, they wanted the torpedo itself.

For this operation—theft of one of the new German torpedoes—the civil servants had a candidate, an expatriate American of French descent called DeRoche, who did not leave France with the other expatriates when the Germans arrived in 1940. DeRoche was big and burly, a great fat jolly fellow, a Falstaff with a black eye patch who worked as a film editor at the movie studios in Joinville. It was there that Leila recruited him. "I've been waiting for the Resistance to come around," he'd said. "Now give me a job."

Ricard went back to Saint-Nazaire, and he and DeRoche watched the naval base from a rooftop, and waited for a diversion. It came on a drizzling April evening. That night the RAF hit hard. A squadron of British Stirling bombers appeared, their arrival greeted by massed anti-aircraft fire, floods of red tracer rounds streaming into the night sky. One of the RAF bombers was hit, its engine caught fire and, by firelight, parachutes were seen drifting toward the sea.

Sitting in the passenger seat of a panel truck, Ricard felt his heart pounding, but, when the action started, the fear melted away. Ricard drove the truck up to the gate, showed the guard his stolen entry permit, and the man waved him through. Off a dirt road on the other side of the gate, he found the metal shed where the torpedoes were stored. An armed sentry at the door held up his hand and said, "Halt!" The time for finesse had passed, so DeRoche took a .45 automatic from his leather jacket and shot the guard, who fell to his knees. DeRoche shot him twice more, and he rolled onto his back.

DeRoche and Ricard ran to the door of the shed, found it padlocked, but it took only one kick from the powerful DeRoche: the door splintered and swung open. Inside the shed, Ricard's flashlight illuminated rows of torpedoes strapped to hand trucks. Ricard chose one, but he could barely move it, then DeRoche took over and wheeled the torpedo past the guard's body and put it into the panel truck.

Early the next morning, two Gestapo officers drove up to the shed, where a French detective, called Guarini, and a German naval officer were waiting for them. Guarini, a Corsican with dark complexion and black hair, did the police work: identified the dead guard, found the three shell casings and put them in a paper bag, and searched the immediate area for other clues. He looked for tire tracks on the dirt road, but the dirt was dry and hard and the vehicle had left no trace on its surface.

As the Gestapo officers watched him work, one of them said, "What calibre?"

"They used a forty-five," Guarini said.

"An American weapon?" the officer asked.

"Maybe," Guarini said. "But forty-five calibre automatics are manufactured all over Europe. Still, if I had to guess, I'd say this particular weapon was the Browning model carried by the American military."

The officer took a notepad from his pocket and wrote down **Killer used an American .45 automatic.** Then he said, "So we might assume that the killing was done by a Resistance cell in France—the Resistance is partial to slow, heavy bullets that stop a victim in his tracks."

Guarini hesitated, then said what the German officer wanted to hear: "I think it's a good possibility. Who else would steal a torpedo? It's not something you can sell." Then he called over to the German naval officer, "Only one torpedo gone?"

The naval officer said, "Looks like it. The itinerary will have to be examined, but I suspect that only one torpedo was taken."

"So we have here the operation of an intelligence service, likely a British intelligence service—they're the ones who worry about convoys and torpedoes, and they know our submarines are based in Saint-Nazaire," the Gestapo officer said. "And it has to be a local operation, our shore surveillance did not pick up a boat landing."

"A few weeks ago," Guarini said, "one of our spies reported that a torpedo detonator was taken by one of the Polish laborers who work at the factory where the detonators are manufactured. We don't know what became of it."

The Gestapo officer grimaced. "Goddamn Poles," he said. "They won't give up. They stole a detonator, then they came back for the torpedo. What's next? A submarine?"

THE
SAFE
HOUSE

JULY HAD USUALLY BEEN A PLEASANT SEASON IN Paris, sunny and warm, but during the last week of the month, in 1943, temperatures climbed into the nineties, the air humid and still, with no relief at night for a city built of absorbent stone. On the hottest, stickiest nights, the Parisians couldn't sleep—they tried, stripped down and lay still on damp sheets, but soon enough rose and sat by their open windows, smoking cigarettes in the dark. Paul Ricard, sweltering under the slate tiles of his garret roof, made a telephone call, then went off to see his friend Romany, up on the fancy Avenue Bosquet. He found a taxi, wood-fired engine on the roof, and gave the driver the address.

They never got there. On the Rue Saint-Dominique, a taxi hit the front wheel well of Ricard's taxi. Now the drivers cursed each other as a crowd gathered on the street. Ricard sat in the backseat, wiping sweat from his face with a handkerchief, and told himself to be patient: these little accidents happened, now one had happened to him.

Ten minutes later, two policemen appeared. The sergeant in charge told Ricard to get out of the taxi, then watched him carefully as he complied. **Something is wrong.** The idea drifted up from his subconscious and took root.

These weren't Parisian **flics.** The uniform was right, but they didn't quite act like the police he was used to. **Too polite,** he thought, like actors playing police in a play. Parisian police were polite on the surface, but they were ready to hit you with their lead-weighted cape or their **bâton** if you showed defiance. And, somehow, they let you know it.

"Your papers, monsieur."

For a passenger? Well, maybe a witness. **For such a gentle little bump?** Ricard was trying to make something normal of the event, but he couldn't. He handed over his papers, the **flic** took them and walked away. Ricard panicked. Without papers, especially under the occupation, you didn't exist. Ricard ran after the policeman. "My **papers,**" he said.

"I understand, monsieur, come to the Préfecture

tomorrow morning, 116 Rue de Grenelle, and we will return your papers." Followed by the traditional salute: index finger to brim of kepi.

No going to see Romany now, he thought. He headed quickly for home, feeling vulnerable and exposed without his papers.

Back in his garret, Ricard worried and paced. He tried to work on his novel, but he couldn't concentrate. Usually, no matter the trouble, this helped. Transported to another world, where his fictional characters had a life of their own, he left his daily reality and lived in the world he had built for them—a much-easier place to live.

He couldn't stop brooding about the faked accident, and, suddenly, he thought, **I am being prepared.** The Gestapo wanted something from him. What other reason could there be? He was to play a role in some theatre of intrigue they had constructed. So then, how to say no? How to say no without being tortured and shot? And his interior voice wasn't done with him, **You will have to do what they tell you.** Or seem to. Or pretend to.

The following day he went as instructed to the Préfecture. The **flics** were courteous as they handed over his papers. From Ricard, a deep, though silent, sigh of relief. The bastards had scared him.

As he turned to leave the Préfecture, a voice said, "Ricard?"

He turned to face a Gestapo officer who had appeared from an office adjacent to the reception counter. "Step inside," the officer said, holding the door open for him.

Ricard entered the office. "I am Major Erhard Geisler," the officer said. Ricard sat across the desk from the officer. "I am going to give you a chance to help us, and to help yourself."

"Yes?" Ricard said. Then added, "Sir." His heart was beating hard.

"Your residence permit for Paris, may I see it?"

Ricard handed over the document, the officer studied it and said, "I see you keep it up to date."

"I follow the rules, sir," Ricard said.

"Smart fellow," Geisler said. "And you know what happens to those who don't follow the rules." Geisler didn't draw a finger across his throat, he didn't have to, a certain tone in his voice did that job for him.

But Geisler didn't hand the residence permit back; he put it in his desk drawer. "I'll just keep this for a while. If you are stopped at a street control, you can tell them where your residence permit is."

"Won't I be detained?"

"You may well be, but it will all be worked out when the police contact my office. Now, a certain committee has been established, the Union Nationale des Écrivains—the National Writers' Committee—and you've been enrolled as one of its members. The job of the committee is to make sure that writers of all political views are read by French readers. At this time, that isn't the case—writers of the left, that crowd from the Deux Magots, are popular. But Europe is changing and it's time for French intellectuals, among others, to understand that. Now, you have questions?"

"No, sir."

"Then I'll wish you good day."

Ricard had no intention of trying to live in Paris without a permit, and he wasn't going to let these bastards rule his life from a desk drawer. So he visited a specialist in false papers, known as a shoemaker. The shoemaker lived in the Marais, in a small hotel on a square off the Rue de Plâtre. He was an artist, this shoemaker, working at a desk piled with counterfeit rubber stamps, pens, and bottles of the purple ink used by bureaucrats.

Typing Ricard's name on a residence permit, he said, "I've never been so busy, but I'd like to go back to forging checks and documents—this occupation is hard on my nerves."

In fifteen minutes, Ricard was again approved for residence in the city of Paris.

Ricard telephoned Colonel de Roux that afternoon and, the following day, took the train up to Les Andelys. Colonel de Roux met him at the station with a horse and wagon and slowly, crossing and recrossing the Seine, they made their way to the colonel's house. Nadine, the colonel's sheepdog, had come along for the ride, sometimes barking at the cows in the fields, sometimes leaping from the cart to investigate something that interested her, then catching back up to the cart and jumping in.

At the colonel's house they had lunch: a tough chicken stewed in wine with onions and the yellowish curved potatoes known as **rattes.** Over lunch, Ricard told de Roux about the Polish resistance and the German U-boats. De Roux was both delighted and amused. "The Poles go on forever," he said. "They fight back, so the enemies on their borders think twice before they try any nonsense." Then de Roux said, "Do you know the waterways of France, Monsieur Ricard? The canals and the navigable rivers?"

"I don't. The names of most of the rivers, those I know, but, after that . . ."

"It's quite a system, though most people really aren't aware of its extent."

"I believe there may be a lot of canals, a lot of rivers."

De Roux nodded and said, "There are, more than you would imagine. Let's go to my map room and have a look."

August. Now the real heat of the summer arrived and Parisians fled the city, gathered in friends' country houses if they didn't have their own, or stayed at small **pensions**—breakfast and dinner included. Ricard and DeRoche took rooms at one of them, near the village of La Fontaine on the Loire. On a cloudy afternoon, the hotel kitchen prepared a picnic for them, then they rented horses at a local stable and rode along a dirt path by the river. At first, Ricard, very much a city boy, knew he was going to fall off, his legs spread wide in the saddle, but the horse was a gentle beast and used to inexperienced riders, so walked at a slow pace in the summer heat.

There was a boat rental facility at La Fontaine, with a machine shop where they repaired river craft—mostly barges and the tugboats that towed them. They found the proprietor working at a forge, sweat soaking through his shirt as he hammered a bent propeller blade back to its proper shape. The proprietor lifted a welding shield up to his forehead and said, "Gentlemen, what can I do for you?" Lying on a table was his hat, a much-battered and faded naval cap.

"We're staying at La Fontaine," Ricard said.

"August vacation?"

"Yes. It's too hot to stay in Paris." Ricard opened the wicker case that had held their picnic and produced a bottle of white Bordeaux. "Can we offer you a drink?" he said.

"I wouldn't mind," the proprietor said.

DeRoche took a multi-blade knife from his pocket and used the corkscrew blade to open the wine, pouring it into three glasses he took from leather straps that were looped atop the picnic hamper. Ricard lifted his glass, said "Salut," and they drank.

The proprietor closed his eyes for a moment and said, "**Mon Dieu,** that's good." He had a look at the label on the bottle and raised his eyebrows: "Oh, of course," he said. "Grapes from the same estate that bottles Château d'Yquem."

"An old bottle," Ricard said. "Hidden from the Germans."

The proprietor spat on his forge, producing a brief sizzle. "They come here with their French whores, as though they were on vacation."

"And do they patrol the river here?"

"Not really. As the Seine is the great river of Paris, the Loire is the great river of France, the longest river in the country, but it can't be navigated. I mean, look at it."

They looked: a slow trickle of water, maybe two feet deep, worked its way past the gravel islands of the river.

"Tell me, monsieur . . ."

"Pascal."

Ricard and DeRoche shook hands with him and introduced themselves.

"So then," Ricard continued, "all the barge traffic moves on the canals."

"That's how it's always been. Always. Everything moves on the canals, on barges. Wheat and rye, bricks, coal, much of what is produced in the region. Now it goes as far as Lyons, then by rail off to Germany."

"So, the Germans patrol the canals?"

"They try. There's a patrol boat that comes by here, on the canal, once in the early morning, then at dusk."

"And the canals," DeRoche said, "how deep are they?"

"It changes with the season, but around here we say more than eight feet."

DeRoche and Ricard glanced at each other— that was deep enough for a shallow-draft tugboat. Ricard refilled the glasses and, after Monsieur Pascal had taken a sip, he said, "You know, I wasn't born yesterday. The kind of information you're seeking could get you in trouble if you asked the wrong person."

"I don't think you're the wrong person, Monsieur Pascal."

Pascal smiled. "I'm not. My friends and I don't like the Boche. It's nothing official, just a group of Frenchmen, but we keep an eye on what's what here, just in case, someday, somebody wants to know."

"Can you help us with a boat?"

"I would think so. By **help** do you mean engine repair? New sails? I can give you a good price on whatever you want. I live in the village of La Fontaine, everyone knows us Pascals, we've worked the canals for generations. So, what kind of boat do you need?"

"A small tugboat with a shallow draft," Ricard said. "Do you know the people who operate tugboats?"

"I know everybody, tugboat captains included. Of course you need a particular kind of captain, because what you propose sounds to me like a Resistance operation."

"You could call it that," Ricard said.

Pascal thought for a moment. "Some of the captains are political, some not. But I think your best man is known as Bastien, his surname. He's getting on in years, but he fought in the Great War and he's very much a patriot, and he is fearless."

"And where would we find Bastien?"

"The tugboat captains, and the river pilots—canal pilots—are to be found at Nantes, where the river pilots' association has a small office, on the Quai de la Fosse."

Ricard thanked him for the information. Then Pascal said, "What are you going to do with a tugboat?"

"We don't need it for long, a few days will do. So we mean to use it, do what we need to do, then get away."

Pascal shook his head. "What will you be carrying on the tugboat?"

"Certain German equipment—better I don't say more than that."

"Well then, let's go and see your barge captain."

Pascal had the use of an automobile and drove DeRoche and Ricard over to Nantes and the river pilots' office on the Quai de la Fosse. The association was housed in a single room in a creaky wooden building that hadn't yet fallen into the river, but it would get there. Inside, it smelled of strong coffee and tobacco smoke. Bastien turned out to be in his late seventies, with a deeply seamed face and bright eyes with lines at the corners from squinting into the weather at sea. He wore a wool watch cap and smoked smelly little brown cigars.

The three chatted for a time, then Bastien said, "What is it you want towed?"

"We're using it for transport, so it won't tow anything."

Bastien stared at them—what **was** this?

"We have a heavy load, the shape of, say, a torpedo."

"And you want me to take it up into the canal?"

"That's our plan."

"Crazy, my friends, truly crazy, but why not."

The conversation continued for a while, then it was time for Bastien to go to work. They said goodby, and, as Bastien left, he said, "Contact me when you're ready."

DeRoche and Ricard returned their horses and found a train that, with a connection, would take them back to Paris. The provincial waterways departments had been digging barge canals since the 1700s, and, as they moved north in the hot afternoon, the clatter of the train's wheels changed as they crossed the railway bridges. The people who worked the barges also lived on them; sometimes a woman, hanging out washing, would wave at the train, and family dogs barked as it passed above them.

In Paris, on the last day of August, Kasia visited Madame de la Boissière at her apartment, but just as Kasia arrived, a customer showed up, then another. By late afternoon, the two decided to seek privacy at Kasia's room above the stockyards, where, after a glass of wine, Kasia stretched out over Madame de la B.'s knee, took down her panties, and was smartly spanked. Not too hard, not too fast, Madame de la B. was practiced and adept, and accompanied the event with a softly spoken narrative.

The two were lying in Kasia's bed when the telephone rang, and Kasia, pink bottom wobbling as she crossed the room, answered it. At the other end of the line, Teodor, the spy who worked for the civil servants in London, sounded shaky. He suggested a meeting that night, at a café in the Seventh Arrondissement. This was, to Kasia, an alarming telephone call. Contact with Teodor had always been clandestine—but this time he had simply called. Openly. No chalk marks on lampposts, no oblique classified advertisements, no twelve-year-old courier.

Madame de la B., lying in bed with head propped on hand, the two rolls of her stomach sagging on the sheet, wondered about the call but said nothing. Kasia had her mysteries, Madame de la B. knew better than to intrude. The two shared a taxi, which dropped Madame de la B. off at her apartment, then proceeded to the Rue Saint-Dominique. There sat Teodor, with coffee and newspaper, looking around every few seconds.

Kasia didn't like it, told the driver to continue a way down the street, got out, and found herself a vantage point in a doorway. She couldn't be sure, but sensed a trap. Many of the patrons seemed commonplace, but the pairs of large men in summer suits disturbed her. Then one of the men approached a nearby table—again a pair of men— then returned to his table. That was enough for Kasia. This **was** a trap. Teodor had been turned by the Gestapo and was being used as bait.

DeRoche and Ricard had hidden the stolen torpedo in a panel truck, which they'd parked in a garage in Nantes. The owner of the garage didn't like it— he knew there was something dangerous in there, hidden beneath a canvas tarpaulin. He didn't think Ricard and DeRoche were thieves, he thought they were **résistants,** and, if their operation didn't work out, they would bring the Gestapo down on him. Yes, he was a patriot, but his patriotism only went so far—he planned to see the end of the war and to go back to living as he had before the Germans invaded.

But he need not have worried. The following morning, Ricard and DeRoche were back, and drove the truck away in a cloud of gray exhaust smoke. The torpedo had to be moved to a rendez-vous in the middle of France and, with all roads under German surveillance, it had to travel by tugboat, using the Loire canals.

The tugboat carrying the torpedo left at dawn, on the Loire canal that wound its way to Orléans, then to the Rhône, the great river that flowed south to empty into the Mediterranean Sea near the city of Montpellier. Ricard sat against a bollard at the stern of the tugboat. As the sun rose, the leafy branches of oak and chestnut trees formed a canopy above the canal and threw shadows on the still, green water. Around a bend, a flight of starlings took off from the trees and wove patterns in the sky and, now and then, small vees of geese passed overhead. Two hours from Nantes, the canal narrowed, then a village appeared on both banks and a fisherman waved to Ricard from an ancient bridge, perhaps a medieval bridge, built of stone block with arches for boat passage along the waterway. Later, a barge carrying stacked lumber passed Ricard, likely headed for Nantes, a barge hauled by a pair of oxen, who trudged along the tow path encouraged by a young girl with a long switch. It was quiet on the water, only, from time to time, the sound of a passing train on the track that ran beside the river. Otherwise, there was only the thrum of the tugboat's engine.

Just after midday, the tugboat reached the town of La Chebuette and docked at the town's single pier. Following instructions, Ricard found the local hotel and asked the clerk to buzz the room of one Monsieur Dubroc, no doubt an alias. Two men came downstairs. Both were young, and wore eyeglasses and tight beards—to Ricard, they looked like engineers. They all boarded the boat, then Bastien got under way, but not for long. A mile from town they found a narrow channel, water lilies floated on its surface, and its banks were overgrown with high reeds—nobody had been here for a long time.

In the 1920s, there had been a brickyard at the end of the channel where bricks had been fabricated, then loaded onto barges and taken to construction sites along the river. The two men got to work right away; they measured the torpedo, took photographs, removed the detonator, and photographed that as well. "This torpedo is going to England," one of the men said. "But just in case something goes wrong on the way, we'll at least have information about it."

As the tugboat reversed and chugged out of the brickyard, one of the engineers said, "Thank you for your work, Ricard, when the war is over maybe you should get a medal, but I would be surprised if you did. Anyhow, goodby, now it's time for you to return home and forget this ever happened."

Thus, on the twentieth of September, Ricard found himself back in his garret. He stared out at the Rue de la Huchette, as he often did, at the Café La Régence, where local citizens and German occupation troops sat at tables on the **terrasse**, taking the sun on a fine September day. The Investigator, his novel in progress, sat where he'd left it, by his Remington typewriter. He would, he thought, need another two months or so to finish it. Ricard hadn't noticed it at first, but now he saw a scrap of paper on the floor that had obviously been slipped under his door. "Please call me," the note said. It was signed **K.**

Ricard telephoned. "It's Teodor," Kasia said. "He's been captured and turned by the Gestapo, if you meet with him you stand a chance of being arrested."

"How do you know he's been turned, Kasia?"

"He **told** me, he said there was no way out for him, and asked me to have him killed. There were tears in his eyes."

"**Killed?**"

"So he said."

This was, Ricard knew, the way Resistance networks operated. If one of their members became dangerous—and it didn't take much to persuade the leaders they were in danger—they were quick to eliminate the threat. Many people in France died that way in 1943; some innocent, some guilty.

"Are you willing to do such a thing?" Ricard said.

"I suppose so, if I have to. Better that than the Rue des Saussaies." She meant the building used by the Gestapo to interrogate their prisoners. The screams could be heard on the street, and the Parisians found other ways to get where they were going.

Conscious of his open telephone line, Ricard said, "Why don't you come over to my apartment so we can talk?"

"When?"

"Now."

A half hour later, Kasia appeared. She still wore her brown wool suit and tie-up oxford shoes. "I'm not going to kill him; I'm not going to live with that memory," Ricard said.

"What can you do?"

"Get him out of this country. I have a lot of money, American dollars from my friends in London. Can you talk to him, Kasia? Safely? You can't go anywhere near him now."

"I can telephone from a café."

"Quickly. Less than a minute. Before the Germans figure out where the call is coming from."

Kasia nodded.

Later that morning, Ricard visited a travel agency

in the Eighth Arrondissement. There were four desks at the agency, with German officers looking at brochures at two of them. "We are busy, as you see," the travel agent, a middle-aged woman, told him.

"I have a friend who is thinking of taking a voyage," Ricard said.

"Oh yes? And where would the friend like to go?"

"Argentina."

"A long way from here."

"Yes, isn't it."

"Your friend will need an exit visa, and then we'll have to find him space on a ship. South America is a popular destination just now. **Very** popular."

"It must be the local color, the, umm . . ."

"Gauchos."

"Yes, the gauchos, and lots of steaks to eat."

"When does your friend wish to travel?"

"As soon as possible."

"Well, as soon as you show up with the exit visa and his passport, we can write the ticket. Round-trip?"

"One way."

The travel agent nodded. "It will be a long war," she said.

Once again, Kasia and Ricard conferred in Ricard's apartment. "Anything new?" Ricard said.

"Not much. A while back I saw this very attractive woman on the Métro, young, with a shag of blonde hair across her forehead. So yesterday I took the Métro and there she was again. This time I talked to her and I suggested we have lunch together. She liked the idea. I said, 'We could have supper in my little room,' and she seemed to like that idea too. Anyhow, I'm not sure she knows what's going on, but we'll have an intimate conversation, and then we'll see."

"The thrill of the chase," Ricard said.

"Nothing like it."

"What shall we do about Teodor?"

"False papers, that's the only way. Passport, exit visa, and then a ticket to Argentina. Do you know somebody?"

"I do. I'll need the franked photograph from Teodor's passport."

"I'll telephone him from a café. He can leave his passport at The Bookshop and I'll pick it up when I go to work. I'll arrange to be elsewhere when he arrives, we'll have him leave it in a book."

"A Spanish dictionary," Ricard said.

Kasia grinned and said, "The very thing."

A late-September afternoon, the sky sometimes gray, threatening rain, then blue and sunny, with windblown cloud scudding over the city. Ricard left his garret, headed for the Jardin du Luxembourg.

To keep him company in the park he brought along his copy of Eric Ambler's **A Coffin for Dimitrios**. The garden had a central avenue, which led to a pool where kids could sail toy boats, then, to either side, was divided by shrubbery into small private rooms with benches.

Ricard chose one of the rooms and opened his novel. He was at the point where Latimer, the university professor, is talking to Colonel Haki, the Turkish detective in Istanbul. Ricard read with great pleasure—this was his third time through the book, he knew what came next, and he looked forward to it. There were, he thought, good vitamins in this book, nourishing to a writer of spy fiction.

A man appeared at the entry to the shrubbery room and said, "Are you Ricard, the writer? May I join you?"

Ricard moved over on the bench, and the man sat down. He was in his forties, maybe a matinee-idol type when younger, but now his hair was thinning, and worry lines marked his face. He was, Ricard thought, aging quickly. He wore a shaggy mustache, black with gray strands, and had on sunglasses.

"You like your book?" he said.

Ricard nodded.

"Your favorite Ambler?"

"I think so, everything is right; Istanbul, and the Dimitrios character, and his history in the Levant."

"Better than **The Dark Frontier**," the man said. Then he said, "I should tell you I'm called Adrian."

"You're English?"

"I'm a little bit of everything—'Adrian' was somebody else's idea, but it will do for the moment."

Well, he wasn't, by his accent, French, Ricard thought. He didn't sing the language the way the French did, enjoying every word. Yet his French was perfect, the language of a foreigner who was used to it, and likely worked in it. So, who was he?

"Are you surprised I know who you are?" Adrian said.

"Well, there are photographs on my dust jackets."

"I've read them all, by way of getting to know you. They're good, Monsieur Ricard, **The Waterfront Spy**, **The Odessa Affair**, all of them, and you have something in common with Ambler. Your hero is not a detective, not a government agent. Like Ambler's Latimer, he's caught up in the politics of his time. One is sympathetic to Latimer, a rather stodgy college professor thrown into the middle of a secret operation because he writes **romans policiers**, his way of escaping academic publication. That's what makes the Ambler novels good. I grew tired of policeman heroes, Simenon's Maigret and Hercule Poirot, Agatha Christie's detective; I prefer the amateurs, like Latimer. And like you, Monsieur Ricard."

Ricard well knew this contact with a stranger was no accident, and waited for the man called Adrian to reveal the reason for it.

Adrian leaned forward a little and said, "According to my friend Leila and to the people in

London she works for, you did well in Paris, and in Saint-Nazaire. Like Ambler's heroes, you're a committed anti-fascist."

"I always was, all through the thirties, and now, with the occupation, even more so."

"And prepared to work?"

Ricard hesitated. He had only just gone back to living his usual life and took pleasure in it. But he understood that refusing Adrian's offer wasn't really possible. When a war comes to your country, you have to join up. What was Trotsky's quote? "You may not be interested in war, but war is interested in you." Finally, Ricard said, "What do you want me to do?"

"This park feels a little too **public**. Is there somewhere we can go? Maybe a restaurant?"

"There's a restaurant I like, up on the Rue de Richelieu. It's too far to walk, we'll have to take a taxi," Ricard said.

"Let's do that, tell me about the restaurant."

"It's called Maurice. On the street floor they have the usual ration-coupon dishes: turnips, cabbage, animal feed. But they have a black-market restaurant on the second floor."

"A good one?" Adrian asked.

"It is. And expensive."

"And do they serve **steak frites**?"

"Oh yes; yes indeed, they are known for it," Ricard said.

"Then let's go and eat there. Is the steak **au poivre**?"

Ricard nodded.

"It's been a long time since I had a real **steak frites.** I think about it," Adrian said.

Ricard claimed he could tell whether a restaurant was good or not by the smell that reached you as you stepped inside the front door. Up on the second floor, the Restaurant Maurice smelled very good indeed. Ricard and Adrian settled at a table by the window, then peered at the day's menu chalked on a blackboard. For a moment, Ricard considered the **poulet rôti** or the quenelles of pike, then ordered the **steak frites.**

As they waited for their orders to arrive, Adrian said, "Do you know the word **exfiltration?** It's a word used mostly by people in the special services."

"Yes. I know the word," Ricard said. "It means helping someone escape from a hostile area."

"That's what we want you to do. There are fugitives hiding out all over France, our own agents, French agents, and the Poles. Hundreds of agents, all of them used to convey information that can be used to defeat the Reich. We use wireless/telegraph sets to transmit some of this information, but much of it travels by hand, down established escape lines until it reaches Spain and, in time, finds its way to London. These escape lines send the courier from safe house to safe house, all run by people who don't like the Germans or the

Vichy administration. One of our jobs back here is to keep our couriers safe.

"What we want you to do is travel down one of these escape lines. It has a code name, SHEPHERD, assigned by the people in London. This line, like many others, goes from Paris down to Perpignan, then to Spain, in time to the British naval base at Gibraltar. You'll make contact with our agents in Spain and they'll escort you to the base."

Their soup arrived at the table, a **potage de légumes,** warm and thick, colored a rich brown by the lentils used to make it. Ricard ate a spoonful and recalled how the French **believed** in soup— with bread and wine it was all one really needed. "And why the SHEPHERD line?" Ricard said.

"We need to be certain that it isn't penetrated by the Boche."

"And you're not certain now?"

"We're not, but then, we are professionally suspicious. One of the women that ran a safe house for SHEPHERD has disappeared. Now we have reason to believe she was having a love affair, was caught by her husband, then ran away with her lover. They fled . . . we don't know where, but we don't believe that the Gestapo snatched her and made up the story. We **believe,** but we don't **know,** so it needs to be investigated."

Adrian had some more of his soup, then said, "We have a car for you, a Citroën Berline 11, the 1938 model, adapted with a coal-burning engine when the gasoline was sent to Germany. You have official permission to drive it, because you are supposedly a veterinary surgeon, we'll give you the papers."

"I haven't done much driving," Ricard said. "I'm a city boy, but I know how to drive."

"Alright, better if you don't drive. The Boche run snap checks on cars—in the city and in the countryside. We'd prefer that you take the trains, especially the night trains, because the Germans don't like to work at night, so **Kontrols** on those trains are very rare."

"So much for German efficiency," Ricard said.

"That's something of a myth—the Germans like to think of themselves as efficient, but they aren't really. Thank God. Now the normal procedure for a new operative is to send him to Scotland where we have a training base, but in your case we don't have the time. We need an investigator right away, to make sure of the safe houses and the people who have the responsibility of running them."

The waiter took the soup plates away, then brought the **steak frites:** the potatoes gold and crisp, still sizzling from the fryer, and intensely aromatic. On the side, a dish of béarnaise sauce for both steak and **frites.** The dinner stopped conversation for a time—both Adrian and Ricard had been living on wartime diets and they were hungry. After the main **plat,** a green salad, then a fresh pear.

Ricard and Adrian both lit cigarettes as coffees arrived. "Find yourself a safe house," Adrian said.

"You can't do this work from your apartment. A house with a chimney to hold the wire for the wireless/telegraph set. A chimney not visible from the street."

"I'll find something," Ricard said. "How much rent should I pay for it?"

"Whatever it costs," Adrian said. "Speaking of which . . ." He passed Ricard a fat envelope beneath the table. Ricard looked inside and saw American bills in fifty-dollar denominations. "It's five thousand dollars. Convert some of it into occupation francs—for train fares and room rentals—but keep the dollars for bribes. Anyhow, use it as you like and don't scrimp, there's plenty more where that came from."

"Still," Ricard said, "a lot of money."

"It isn't really, because the way we fight these days is with money. That's our weapon."

So, a safe house. Where to look? Years earlier, after leaving his room near the Sorbonne, Ricard had looked for a new place to live. In time he found his garret by chatting with street-market vendors in the **quartier** because these women, toughened and weathered by years of selling vegetables in all seasons, knew everything that went on. "See Madame Cabard," he'd been told, and he had tracked her down at her vegetable stand. She had a friend who owned a building on the Rue de la Huchette, and Ricard, searching for an apartment, soon had a garret. "For an artist, or a poet, it's just right," Madame Cabard said.

Of course, Paris had changed in 1940, and there was now a surplus of apartments for rent. Some had belonged to Jews who'd been rounded up by the police, some had belonged to foreigners— mostly American or British—who'd once upon a time, with money to spare, thought an apartment in Paris was a fine trophy. The war had chased them back home, and now the **For Rent** pages of the newspapers had columns of available apartments, and available houses.

Ricard began by considering the city arrondisse- ment by arrondissement; the streets around his own neighborhood, the Fifth and the Sixth, were full of uniformed Germans, who had replaced the Americans and the British in colonizing the Left Bank—Saint-Germain-des-Prés—student and bohemian Paris. The Seventh remained a bastion of the old, rich families who had lived there for generations. Ricard wanted a neighborhood where strangers weren't so much the subjects of specula- tion and gossip. There were numerous vacant apartments in the Marais, but those had once been Jewish apartments, and the area now felt desolate and abandoned.

To Ricard, the Sixteenth and Seventeenth were occupied by the well-to-do, who cared too much about someone moving in next door. **Perhaps the**

Fourth, Ricard thought, which was technically part of the Marais but was just across the Seine from the Fifth and, until you reached the Eleventh, had the same character. He walked there—it wasn't far from his own street—taking the Pont Marie, then headed for the Place des Vosges, where he found fancy shops and an inviting café, the bistro Ma Bourgogne, which occupied one corner of the park. Here he stopped to have a coffee and a look at the local population.

This was an attractive part of Paris, but there were few Germans about, maybe it wasn't in their guidebooks. The bistro patrons looked shabby and poor, but that was due to the occupation, Ricard knew the **bonne bourgeoisie** when he saw it. This was the proper country for the writer Ricard, he felt at home here, but this was not the proper place for the secret agent Ricard. He wanted, in that role, anonymity, and it wasn't there at Ma Bourgogne—he could have comfortably struck up a conversation with any of the people at the tables on the **terrasse.**

Ricard was tempted by the Tenth, where the two railway stations, the Gare de l'Est and the Gare du Nord, were located. But if agents traveling on any of the escape lines were going to be hidden there, they would be surrounded by German travelers in great numbers, going on, or returning from, leave in Germany. **So,** Ricard thought, **the Tenth won't work.** What he would need was a railway station from which trains headed south, toward Perpignan, then Spain, for agents trying to get out of the country. This meant the Gare de Lyon, in the Twelfth Arrondissement.

Ricard took the Métro to the Gare de Lyon stop and walked up the stairs. Coming out of the station, he saw the span of railroad tracks that emerged from a tunnel, headed for the La Chapelle freight yards, the rails glinting silver in the sunlight. Staring at them, Ricard wanted to be on a train going far away, far away from claustrophobic, occupied Paris. How he'd loved his city. Before the war. Now it was a prison.

Well, tant pis, he thought. Too bad. Walking north from the station on the Rue de Bercy, he was close to the Seine, could see barges being worked up the river. Here he came upon the Rue Crémieux, a sullen street with a couple of cheap hotels. In the middle of the block, he found a narrow—two rooms wide—building, plastered in darkening tan stucco, with a small **boulangerie** on the ground floor that had a FOR RENT sign in the window. He entered the shop, bought a demi-baguette, asked about the building, and was told to see the notary at his office on the next block. One Monsieur Luc, who turned out to be a talkative gent with white hair. Monsieur Luc paged through a dossier and said, "It's been vacant for a long time."

"It's a good place for me," Ricard said. "I'll take it."

After hesitating, Monsieur Luc said, "Monsieur, you don't . . ." He didn't finish, but Ricard knew where he was going. Ricard didn't look like the sort of person who would live in such a place. "I need a building to store equipment," he said, then paid two months' rent in occupation francs, signed a one-year lease, and Monsieur Luc gave him the key.

Ricard returned to the building and, after a struggle with the lock, went inside. The interior was empty of furniture and smelled of dust and mold. A narrow wooden staircase led up to the second floor, one room right, one left. The floorboards were warped, now bare wood and gray with age; and the walls, painted white a long time ago, were stained. On the top floor, a chimney rose through the roof. At the base of the chimney was an opening with a square black stain on the floor where a small stove had stood. Looking out the window, Ricard saw that he was above a courtyard with some kind of workshop, one story high, opposite the window. Ricard cranked the window open and smelled fresh varnish—perhaps they made furniture in the shop. Closing the window, he thought about actually living in the building, a safe house had to have a guardian.

Someone would have to live there, to take care of agents on the move or fugitives on the run. Find food for them—they would need ration cards, but these were easily forged—and have a bed for them to sleep in. Looking at the chimney, Ricard thought that a W/T wire could be run up the inside—as long as a heater wasn't being used. It was now late October, people were walking around barely heated apartments in their overcoats, perhaps, he thought, he could find some thick blankets.

Heading back toward the Métro, Ricard chewed the end off his demi-baguette. It was dreadful, the same consistency as cotton, baked with occupation flour. He threw the remainder of the bread into the street, where it was set upon by the local pigeons.

10 October, the Gare de Lyon. Ricard began his journey down the SHEPHERD escape line by taking the night train to Troyes, some hundred and ten miles southeast of Paris. At the station, the waiting room was half full and barely lit, so that some of the travelers faded into the shadows. The train was late, according to the Roman numeral clock on the wall. This was confirmed by the appearance of a ticket clerk, who used a rag to erase 23:30—the railways ran on twenty-four-hour time, military time—and then chalked in 00:30. The trip down to Troyes would take two hours or so; Ricard would be there at two in the morning.

Ricard looked around the room. Were there British agents on the move in here? German operatives hunting them? Two gendarmes—army uniforms and red kepis, flat-topped hats with horizontal brims—entered the room and moved among the benches, asking to see papers. Not for all the travelers, only some of them. They stopped and stood over Ricard, one of them saying, "Your papers, monsieur." Ricard did as he asked, and the gendarme held up a typed list and compared Ricard's name to the ones on his paper. He took his time, was careful, and in no hurry, and Ricard grew tense as the gendarme searched.

What had Teodor told the Gestapo before Ricard had him sent off to Argentina? His name? Likely not. If Teodor had done that, Ricard would have been arrested. Or did they decide to wait? To follow him and see who he met and what he did? The Gestapo certainly operated in that way. The gendarme handed Ricard back his passport and exit visa, then took a long look at him. **Your name isn't on this list, but I'm sure we both know it's on some list.**

It was almost midnight when Ricard heard the train pulling slowly into the station, and he walked out on the platform. When the train hissed to a stop, Ricard saw that it was wet, water running down the sides of the cars. It had apparently come through a rainstorm on its way to Paris. At one end of the platform, a large group of Wehrmacht troopers were waiting at the first car. As with the Métro, German soldiers had their own private car.

Where, Ricard wondered, were they going? They were in full combat dress, with heavy packs on their backs and rifles slung on their shoulders. As Ricard watched, they smoked nervously and talked among themselves in low voices. Wherever it was, they clearly weren't happy to be going there. Maybe Russia, with not much chance of ever returning home. Or, maybe, it was North Africa, to fight against British forces, scheduled to invade Italy once the North African coast was secured. The war was changing, Ricard thought. The Allies were, eventually, who knew when, going to win.

It was dark on the train, Ricard found a seat in a first-class compartment—the Germans were very conscious of class distinctions, and rarely checked the first-class passengers. When a woman with a child looked through the glass partition, Ricard rose and gave up his seat, and stood in the aisle, his canvas satchel between his feet. As the train was about to leave, an older woman, gray-haired, well dressed, stood next to him. "Do you always ride the night trains?" she said.

"Now and then," Ricard said. "When there's no other way."

"Are you getting off at Troyes?"

"I am."

"Nice little town, Troyes. Center of trade routes, long ago. You have family there?"

"No. Going to see a friend."

From the woman, a knowing smile. "Always

good to see 'a friend.' Love makes the world go round."

"That's true," Ricard said. Was this woman just an old busybody? Or was there more to it?

"You'll have to take a taxi at the station, unless you're being met."

"Well, I'm not being met."

"Perhaps we can share a taxi. Where does your friend live, in Troyes?"

"I have the address in my bag, I don't remember it."

"You don't?"

"No, I don't."

"You could get it out, that way we might share a taxi."

"Maybe later," Ricard said. This woman was more than a busybody. Someone had sent her to talk to him and find out what he was doing. His heart sank; was there no end to this? He wanted to help Adrian and he'd been lucky so far. But the enemy was relentless—after he eluded this woman, he would be approached again.

At the Troyes station, there were two taxis waiting. Ricard took the first, and asked the driver to go to the commercial hotel he'd been told to use. The driver was a young man, likely the son of the man who owned the taxi and drove it most of the time. After going a few blocks, he said, "That other taxi is following us, monsieur. Someone you know?"

"Someone I don't want to know."

"Ah, yes, that occurred to me. Shall I lose him?"

"Please," Ricard said.

"That will cost extra, we'll burn up more fuel."

"I'll be happy to pay."

The driver sped up, as much as he could—the coal-driven cars could go no faster than forty-five miles an hour—so the driver made up for it by taking Ricard, and whoever was following him, into the old, medieval section of the city, near the cathedral. In a labyrinth of narrow streets, the driver turned left, then right, folding his outside-view mirror flat against the window and taking an alley that seemed too narrow for an automobile. In time, no headlights behind them, they arrived at the hotel.

The chase left Ricard overexcited and tense and, once in his room at the hotel, he couldn't sleep. Music had always calmed him, so he turned the radio on and found a woman vocalist fronting a swing band, "Gonna take a sentimental journey, gonna set my heart at ease." This worked, and soon enough Ricard drifted into a dreamless sleep.

In the morning, Ricard found a café and telephoned the safe house, a doctor's office. This was an extremely important rule, always telephone a safe house before going there, and use the coded protocol:

"Hello, is Michel there?"

"You mean Roland," the doctor said.

"Yes, Roland. Can you see a patient this morning?"

"I believe I can."

If he'd said, "You'll have to wait, I have many patients this morning," it meant that the Germans were there.

According to Adrian, doctors' offices were much-favored sites for the civil servants in London; a doctor's office received calls from many different numbers, messages could be left for other agents, and whoever was bugging the line would not be able to determine which calls had to do with escape lines, as long as the caller was faithful to the use of opaque language.

Ricard took a taxi there and met with the doctor, a graying man in a white coat with a stethoscope hanging around his neck. He showed Ricard to an unused examination room where a young couple was spending the night. The room was empty; the couple, according to the doctor, had hidden in a closet when they'd heard the tap on the door. Back in his office, the doctor said, "They are following the rules." In a safe house, agents were never seen. They had to wait, silent and out of sight, until they were sent on to the next safe house on the escape line.

When they'd returned to the office, the doctor said, "It's hard on them, having to follow the rules.

They're fighting the war, they want their hands on guns and explosives, but once on the escape line, their worst enemy is boredom."

"Is there anything you need?" Ricard said.

"It would be nice to have some books, reading makes the time pass."

"Don't you have a bookshop in Troyes?"

"We do. Or, rather, we did. The people who own it now are faithful to Vichy, or worse, and they have filled their shelves with fascist tracts and propaganda."

"What would you like?" Ricard asked.

"Escapist literature. Historical novels and detective stories, novels about life at sea, or the Napoleonic Wars, or fantasies. I had a good collection of Saint-Exupéry—**Night Flight** and **The Little Prince** and others—but they fell apart, too much reading."

"I'll see what I can do," Ricard said.

The next stop on the SHEPHERD escape line was at a beauty shop, the Salon Lolotte, on the Rue Candolle in the town of Orléans. After the telephone protocol, Ricard went to see the safe house, a spare room above the salon. Entering the salon, Ricard found a row of women sitting patiently beneath chrome hair dryers, the whir of their fans loud in the small shop.

Ricard found Lolotte at work, cutting a woman's hair. She was, Ricard thought, properly named,

Lolotte a nickname for a merry and fun-loving woman. Lolotte herself had carrot-colored hair, was fat and blowzy, red faced, and coarse. Ricard had identified himself by the protocol and asked to see the spare room. He waited while she finished her haircut, then was taken up to the spare room, where two agents were having lunch.

Back in the shop, Lolotte said, "Well, they keep coming . . ."

"Yes, we're grateful for your help."

"You people could be a little more grateful, you know."

"Oh yes? What do you mean?"

"I mean money. That's what **grateful** means, **mon ami.**"

"Did they offer to pay you, when you started out?"

"Not a sou. I'm supposed to do this to help fight the Germans, but food for your agents, or whatever they are, isn't free. And I'm putting myself in danger, that's worth something."

"I'll try to help you, Lolotte," Ricard said. "I have some money with me and I'll bring it over later today." It wasn't so unusual to help the guardians of safe houses, but Ricard had the feeling he was being blackmailed. Still, he wasn't going to argue with her.

"Don't forget," she said, sulky and demanding. "All I have to do is drop a word in someone's ear and, pouf, there goes your safe house and whoever happens to be staying here. I've seen some rough types, you can believe that."

"I know," Ricard said. "Some of our agents are former soldiers."

"One of 'em had his eye on me, meant to have my pussy. He wasn't so bad looking, and my husband died years ago, the little bastard, so I figured here's my new beau, but then he settled on petite Suzette. **Mignonne**"—cute—"that one, with her sweet little nose and pointy tits. One of my hairdressers. She saw this rough type and looked at him that way and began wagging her little behind. So much for Lolotte!"

"What happened to her?"

Lolotte laughed, more like a snicker than a laugh. "**Her?** She's long gone, petite Suzette. Well, I had to say something, didn't I? She was the one who ran the safe house, and when your people didn't hear from her they sent somebody to see what was going on, and that's what I told him."

"Madame Lolotte, what really happened here?"

"Someone, I can't imagine who, betrayed her, and the Gestapo sent one of their cars around. But she ran out the back door and I never saw her again. The Gestapo questioned me, but I didn't tell them anything. They took a long time, a real grilling, but in the end I persuaded them that petite Suzette was in it by herself. I expect they are still looking for her."

"What did you tell them about Suzette?"

"Only that she said she was going to shoot a German. I didn't dare to tell them about the room, or the agents, then they would've taken me away."

True to his word, Ricard brought a thousand occupation francs to the shop later that day. Lolotte was mollified. "Now that's the way to do business," she said.

Ricard resumed his inspection tour: to a cobbler in Bourges, then to a mansion, where the safe house was run by an eighty-year-old couple, in Limoges. Next he visited a farm run by two widowed sisters, husbands gone in the 1914 war, outside Périgueux; then to a small **épicerie**, grocery store, in a village near Agen; to a draper in Toulouse; finally to a bookshop in Perpignan, where the Pyrenees mountain border of Spain was visible from the train station.

With one exception, Ricard thought, these were good and honorable people. They ran escape lines and kept safe houses because they hated the Boche, and they knew what would happen to them if the Gestapo discovered what they were doing, yet they persisted in the face of danger. The Gestapo could be stupid, but they could also be cunning. They set traps for the agents that spied, stole secrets, cut telephone lines, and assassinated German officers. In one case, the Gestapo set up their own escape line, north of Paris, and arrested agents who thought they were headed to Spain.

As planned, Ricard was scheduled to meet with Adrian at the bookshop in Perpignan. This was owned by a gentle couple in middle age, the man with a white beard, who were virtual godparents to young students, struggling writers, communists, intellectuals, whoever needed the consolation of books. They had a carpenter friend, a veteran of the army, and he built them a clever bookcase, which slid aside to reveal a second bookcase. In the first, they stocked the shelves with children's books, lives of the saints, and lengthy tomes that offered the reader ancient history, theology, and science. In the hidden bookcase, one would find the forbidden fruit: Steinbeck, Hemingway, Gide, Sartre, Simone de Beauvoir, François Villon, and Karl Marx. All of these deemed enemies of fascism, their books among those burned by the Nazis in 1933. Officers from the Propagandastaffel had visited the shop, found the couple mildly dotty but not dangerous.

The carpenter who had built the secret bookcase had also designed a secret door, hidden by panels, in what had once been a wine cellar and was now a safe house. The couple brought Ricard down there, said, "Your friend is waiting for you," pressed one of the panels, and there was Adrian.

The couple left them to talk and went back upstairs. "Well," Adrian said, "now you've seen the SHEPHERD line."

"I have seen it, one end to the other, it took me ten days."

"And that's only one of many, there are dozens of others, all over France."

"I had no idea," Ricard said.

"Well, it's what the British can do, right now, send agents to organize resistance, bring coastal raiding parties in by submarine, and bomb the Reich. 'Set Europe ablaze,' as Churchill puts it. Did you find anything amiss?"

"There is a problem, I think, in Orléans. I had to bribe a woman known as Lolotte, who owns the beauty salon. She threatened to betray the woman who ran the safe house."

Adrian was silent for a moment, then said, "Explicitly?"

"Yes. I gave her money, so she's content."

"For the moment," Adrian said.

"Yes, for the moment."

"Well, people like that don't stop. Once they realize they can blackmail somebody, they come back for more."

"I believe she will, that's who she is."

"The line runs through Orléans, we can't change that."

"And the woman?"

"She is my responsibility," Adrian said. "I have to consider her a real threat."

Ricard nodded, and lit a cigarette.

"I imagine you're tired," Adrian said.

Ricard shrugged. "That doesn't matter."

"I want you to check the border crossing, then you can get back on the trains and go home."

·

The following morning, Ricard left Perpignan and took a very slow, two-car local up into the mountains, to the village of Latour-de-Carol, north of the town of Bourg-Madame. At the edge of the village he found a park that lay a few hundred yards from the actual frontier. There was no border station, nobody was entirely sure where the border actually was, and neither the French nor the Spanish residents really cared. Here, on Sunday afternoons, local people from both countries mingled for a few hours until it was time to go home for dinner. Agents coming down the SHEPHERD line joined the residents, met Spanish couriers, and simply walked into Spain.

By the time Ricard got on the train, to make his way, eventually, back to Paris, he was cold—it was autumn—and tired. Spent. The journey down the escape line had exhausted him, though he hadn't realized it at the time. Too many nights on trains, too many people to size up, too much anxiety about being watched or followed, too much shadowy danger in the world of escape lines and safe houses. Headed back to Paris, he broke the rules and took sleeping compartments on express trains—Adrian had given him money, he used it.

And slept well. Beyond well, a dead sleep interrupted only by stops at railway stations. **This is the cure for insomnia,** he thought. The steady beat of train wheels on rails knocked him close to unconscious. At last, Paris, his garret, and, lying on his bed, he exhaled, as though for the first time in days.

Meanwhile, Adrian had made arrangements to solve the difficulty with Lolotte.

The Prestige Taxi Company was located in a garage in an industrial suburb of Orléans. Two men, known as Jules and Henri, met there on the afternoon of 14 November. Jules was tall, had thinning black hair, and a permanent five o'clock shadow, which made him look evil. Which he was. Henri was chubby and pink, baby faced, and had grown a mustache, which made him look like a baby with a mustache. Before the war, Jules had worked as a merchant seaman, Henri as a clerk in a government office, then, with the fall of France in 1940, both men had fled to London to join de Gaulle, and had then been recruited by the British Special Operations Executive, the SOE, for clandestine work in France.

They had met before; now they were in Orléans to do a job for the civil servants. "Are you the driver?" Henri said. "Or is it me?"

"You drive," Jules said. "I'll be the passenger."

They then bribed the dispatcher, who found them a dependable taxi and made sure there was enough coal in the bins beneath the taxi's wheel wells.

They drove out of the garage and found the Rue Candolle, and the Salon Lolotte, then they circled the block and parked a hundred feet from the beauty shop. And waited. Henri drummed his fingers on the steering wheel, Jules smoked a Balto cigarette.

A few minutes after seven in the evening, Lolotte emerged from her salon, locked the door, and headed down the street. She wore a bright green coat and a matching hat with a feather, setting off her carrot-colored hair.

"There she is," Henri said.

Jules climbed out of the backseat and caught up with Lolotte. He put an arm around her shoulders and said, "Lolotte, it's Jules, don't you remember me?"

Lolotte, startled, said, "Who? I'm not sure I . . ."

Those were her last words, because Jules reached around and, revolver in hand, shot her in the heart. Then, to make sure, shot her again, in the left temple. That was the end of Lolotte. And the Orléans safe house was once again safe.

SOLITAIRE

KASIA CALLED RICARD. "I'VE MET SOMEONE," SHE said. "I'm going to a club tonight, why don't you meet me there? I'll buy you a drink, and tell you all."

"Which club?"

"It's called Le Coup de Foudre. It means 'the lightning bolt' "—love at first sight.

Ricard arrived at seven and found the club, in a cellar, somewhere out in the wilds of the Ninth Arrondissement. When Ricard came in the door, all eyes were on him—who is this in our private playground? A few men there but mostly women, all ages, wearing black, two or three of them smoking cigarettes in ivory holders, it reminded him of Berlin in the twenties.

Kasia showed up right away, wearing her worker's-cap/lace-up-boots outfit. Before she sat down, she kissed Ricard on both cheeks. Then she ordered brandies, quickly drank the first one, and dawdled with the second.

"You seem to be in a good mood," he said.

"I had dinner with the bunny rabbit last night." Ricard was perplexed. "The girl with the blonde shag across her forehead," she explained. "I told you about her. I saw her on the Métro and invited her to supper in my room. And she showed up! I worried about that, but there she was, in a dress that showed everything and sexy shoes.

"I cooked us a dinner on my hot plate—an omelet, that's about what I can do, bread, and a bottle of wine. With an assignation, you know, you don't want a heavy meal beforehand. **Afterwards,** that's the time to eat. Then we sat on my bed—there's nowhere else to sit—and I began to rub her back. She was telling me her life story, as one does, went to such and such lycée, up in the Sixteenth where she grew up. Papa was in the chemical business, obviously they were rich. But she wasn't ready to get married and all of that, traveled for a time, before the war, you know, Rome and Venice, Capri, the usual. Then she lived at home until she had to do something, so she got a job teaching at her old lycée, then moved to one closer to the center of the city, where she had to take the Métro, and there I happened to see her, and I liked her right away, so I took that Métro a few times and, lo and behold, there she was and I invited her to dinner.

"Still rubbing her back, I kissed her. She was reluctant at first, then she began to like it and kissed back. Took a little more time, but I got her dress off. What is it about rich girls' bodies? Is it all the tennis they play? Ballet lessons? Anyhow, she was ravishing. Finally I stripped her, little hesitations on the way, of course, but off it all came. Then she sat on the edge of the bed and gave me a very shy, very timid smile. **So,** I thought, **first time with a woman for the bunny rabbit.** I stood in front of her and took off all my clothes. And her eyes never left me, she was rapt.

"Then came the serious part, kissing on the mouth leads to kissing on the breasts, you know? Then down from there. Leisurely, at first, you know?"

"I know, Kasia."

"God! Ricard! She was so loud when she came, the whole building must have heard her! What a girl, Ricard, I think I'm in love."

"I'm glad for you, **mon amie,**" Ricard said. He offered Kasia a cigarette, took one for himself, then lit both and said, "Does she have a name?"

"Denise," Kasia said, lingering on the name, in love with the sound of it.

"She makes you happy, that's obvious."

"That isn't the word for what she makes me."

"So, you'll see her again?"

Kasia nodded, with a knowing smile. "We're going to meet at a hotel, tomorrow night, it's the Grand Hôtel, by the opéra."

"Fancy," Ricard said. "And the restaurant's a good one."

Kasia said, "What will I wear?"

"You'll find something."

"Oh, I will, I'll go to Madame de la Boissière."

A thin woman in black approached the table and said to Kasia, "The band is just starting up, care to dance?" Then she turned to Ricard and said, "You don't mind, do you?"

Ricard gave Kasia a complicit look and said, "I was just leaving."

Room 406, the Grand Hôtel. Kasia had spent some money at Madame de la Boissière's private boutique and wore a cream-colored silk blouse with the top two buttons open and wide-legged wool trousers. It was a thin shirt. Kasia wore no bra and her small breasts were evident beneath the silk fabric. Denise answered her knock immediately, wearing a heavy, bittersweet fragrance and a diaphanous nightdress that fell, just barely, to the tops of her thighs. Kasia kissed her on both cheeks, then on the lips. "You look wonderful, bunny rabbit," she said.

Denise turned in a circle for her and said, "Pretty, no?"

"Mmm."

"I had a bottle of wine sent up, may I pour you a glass?" Kasia nodded, Denise poured a glass of red wine for each of them, then raised her glass and said, "To our time together." Kasia had a sip, the wine was much better than anything she was used to. She walked to the window and, looking down, saw a crowd entering the opera house, some of the women were with German officer escorts. A poster by the opera door said, TONIGHT: OFFEN-BACH, LA BELLE HÉLÈNE. There was more, but the print was too small for Kasia to read from a distance.

Denise had come up behind her and put her arm around Kasia's shoulders; Kasia covered Denise's hand with her own and said, **"Ma biche."** My darling.

"You're sweet," Denise said.

The wine had been served with a basket of buttered little toasts. Kasia had one, then another, then a third. "Merde," she said. "They know how to make toast here."

"Le Grand," Denise said. "The best of everything."

Denise sat on the edge of the bed and patted the space beside her and, as Kasia sat down, turned off the lamp on the night table. That must have been a signal, because the door opened and two men entered, both holding automatic pistols. The leader had fair hair, was a short man, and not happy about it, stood with his chest thrust out and chin held high, and had a fat, sullen face, an angry face. "I am called Vozki; Kasia, put your hands behind your back." As he started to tie her wrists with twine he said, "And that's Simon." Simon was thin and placid looking, with silver-rimmed eyeglasses. There was, Kasia thought, something very wrong with him, as though he lived in another world, his eyes unfocused, a slack smile on his lips.

Vozki looked around the room and found Kasia's pea jacket, draping it across her shoulders so that her bound wrists could not be seen. "Now let's go downstairs and walk through the lobby. Don't cry out, or I will give you the beating of your life."

"What are you going to do with me?" Kasia said.

"Take you to another hotel where you will be under guard." Kasia tried to figure out who Vozki was; where did he come from? But she couldn't. He'd floated up to the surface from the seamy underside of Europe and made his way to Paris— one more predator in the City of Light. Simon was apparently French, at least his name was pronounced in the French fashion.

Still sitting on the edge of the bed, the bunny rabbit was crying, silently, with two tears rolling down her cheeks. "Forgive me, Kasia," she said. "I was forced to betray you." Kasia stared at her and said nothing; she had been led by desire to capture and was too angry to speak.

As Kasia was walked through the lobby,

well-dressed Parisians were all around her, cigarettes in hand, smiling, laughing, posing, making brilliant conversation. They likely noticed Kasia and her keepers, but decided not to notice them—they were simply an oddity that required a glance and a look away. One of the German officers stared briefly, but he was going to the opera and these people, whoever they might be, were beneath him.

There was a car waiting in front of the hotel, a Peugeot that ran on gasoline, not on coal. **Which means,** Kasia thought, **that this Vozki creature is important.** The two men laid Kasia facedown on the backseat, then Vozki drove the car and Simon sat beside him. "The twine is too tight," Kasia said, thinking she might get away as Simon tried to retie her.

"It's not for long," Vozki said.

For some twenty minutes, Vozki drove quickly through the thin traffic, then stopped. The two men helped Kasia from the car, pea jacket draped over her shoulders. Kasia saw that the hotel was called Le Briand, a common second-class commercial hotel. Inside, at the desk, stood an unsmiling blonde woman in SS uniform. She looked like one of those female athletes, in shorts and sleeveless tops, one saw in German newsreels, exercising with a heavy medicine ball. Vozki greeted her in German and she responded briefly. As Kasia was taken upstairs, she realized that the Germans had taken over this hotel for their own personal use.

This puzzled her. Why had they not taken her to some Gestapo office? If not the Gestapo, then who had kidnapped her?

At the beginning of the occupation, Vozki had gone into business, kidnapping people who were **résistants** and selling them to the German security services. At nine in the morning, Vozki drove to the Avenue Kléber and rolled to a stop in front of the Hôtel Majestic, an occupation command center. On the fourth floor of the hotel he found the office of his business associate, SS-Sturmbannführer (Major) Erhard Geisler. Geisler was a pear-shaped man who wore clear-frame plastic eyeglasses, his exterior bland and placid. He was no street thug, rather a man who signed papers ordering arrests, transport to concentration camps, or immediate execution. Vozki stood in front of Geisler's desk, gave the stiff-armed salute, and said, "Heil Hitler." Geisler responded but did not invite Vozki to sit down.

"Herr Vozki," the major said. "What have you got for me?"

"A young woman, Polish, I believe, called Kasia."

Gerhard took from a drawer a thick sheaf of typewritten pages, his list of Paris residents who were suspected of Resistance activity. After finding Kasia's name, he studied the paragraph next to it, then said, "Where is she?"

"In a room at the Hôtel Briand."

"She's not someone I would buy, not as a single unit."

"Then . . . ?"

"She works with a partner, a writer called Paul Ricard. He was known to the English spy Teodor. We'll buy both of them if you can find Ricard."

Vozki wanted to argue but thought better of it. "I will try, Major," he said.

"Then that will be all," Geisler said.

Back at the Briand, Vozki went to the room where Kasia was being held, seated in a chair with her hands tied behind her. Vozki took Simon aside, described his meeting with Geisler, and said, "We will turn this into an opportunity. I'm going to telephone Ricard."

He went down to the reception desk and found Ricard's number in a city telephone directory.

When the phone rang in Ricard's garret he was hard at work on **The Investigator**—a scene where Valois, the arson investigator, confronts the owner of the Roumanian factory. Annoyed at the interruption, he almost didn't answer, then did. "Hello?"

"Monsieur Ricard?"

"Yes."

"I am known as Vozki, I specialize in the capture

of fugitives of interest to the Occupation Authority, and I am calling to tell you that we have taken your friend Kasia and are holding her for ransom. Otherwise, she goes to the Gestapo."

Ricard had to catch his breath, then said, "Ransom. How much do you want?"

"We feel your friend is worth five thousand American dollars. Are you disposed to help her? Or shall I telephone the Gestapo?"

Kasia was no fugitive, Ricard thought, unless the Gestapo decided she was. But he wasn't going to argue with this Vozki person. "Very well," Ricard said. "I'll pay the ransom, but it will take a day or so for me to collect that much money."

"Today is the tenth of November," Vozki said. "Shall we say the fifteenth?"

"Alright, where do I find you?"

"Stay home on the morning of the fifteenth and you'll receive a telephone call. We'll tell you then where to go."

"I'll have to see her," Ricard said, "and make sure she's unharmed."

"Don't worry about that," Vozki said. "Just get the money and all will be well." He hung up, then went back upstairs where Simon was waiting. "This will work," he said, greatly pleased with himself. "We'll collect twice and be paid for the writer as well as the Polish girl."

"You're a very smart fellow," Simon told him.

"Well, that's your good luck," Vozki said.

"She's a pretty girl, Kasia is, why don't we put her on the bed and then, when I'm done, it's your turn."

"Leave her alone, Simon. That kind of thing can come back and hurt you."

"I don't see how." Simon was clearly not convinced, and when Vozki went out to do an errand, he sat on the bed next to Kasia's chair and put a hand on her knee. Kasia moved away and said, "Leave me alone, **conard**."

"Now, now. Don't be like that. Here we have some time together, let's make the most of it."

"Let's not," Kasia said.

He reached out, grabbed Kasia by the neck with one hand, and, with the other, began to stroke her breasts. Kasia wriggled free and swore at him. He laughed, then knelt in front of her and tried to force her knees apart. Kasia's foot fitted nicely in the throat area below Simon's chin, and the kick was powerful enough to send him sprawling on his backside. "Ho, a minx!" he said. "You like to fight before you do it? I know the type." He stood, took a gravity knife from his pocket, and let the blade fall free, then turned it so it gleamed in the lamplight.

"You'll get no ransom if you cut me up," Kasia said, voice level. "Nobody buys damaged goods."

Simon stared at her a moment, not sure how to get what he wanted.

"Now go find someone else to pester," Kasia said. Simon muttered something to himself and put the knife back in his pocket. "Your friends better come up with the money," he said. "Or I'll finish what I started."

Ricard met with Adrian at a café. "Kasia has been kidnapped, this man called Vozki is going to sell her to the Gestapo unless I pay him five thousand dollars."

Adrian thought for a time, then said, "Pay in person?"

"Yes. That's what he said. The money must be paid in two days."

"So there will come a time when you, Kasia, and five thousand dollars will be in the same place. Do I have that right?"

Ricard said he did.

Adrian sighed. "Ricard, forgive me, but has it ever occurred to you that you're not cut out for this business?"

"Many times."

"Where will this happen?"

"They will telephone on the morning of the fifteenth."

"Very well, here's what you're going to do."

On the morning of the fifteenth, Ricard was waiting by his telephone when it rang. "Yes?"

On the other end of the line, Vozki said, "Do you have the money?"

"Not yet. A friend will help me, but the meeting has to be out near his bank—he won't carry that much money around the city, he says it's too dangerous."

"Where does he want to meet?"

"On the Impasse du Ruisseau."

"Where the hell is **that**?"

"Out in Montreuil. His bank is on the next street."

"No," Vozki said firmly. "We'll set the place and time."

Adrian had warned Ricard, had told him he would have to gamble. Ricard said, "Then there's nothing I can do about it."

From Vozki, a long silence while the telephone line hissed. "Well, that's too bad. I'll have to contact the Gestapo. They'll do the paying."

"Not that much," Ricard said.

Again, Vozki paused, but his greed for a double payment was irresistible, and he knew that Ricard's assumption about the Gestapo was correct. "Say again the place," he said.

"The Impasse du Ruisseau. The time is nine at night."

"Then it's set," Vozki grumbled, very much displeased.

Adrian was standing next to Ricard and, as Ricard hung up, Adrian said, "Did he buy it?"

"I think so."

•

Adrian sent a telegram to the Prestige Taxi Company in Orléans, asking Jules and Henri, the **résistants** who had executed the salon owner Lolotte, if they would do a job in Paris. A few hours later they responded, the answer was yes, they liked working for Adrian, he paid immediately and paid well. The two took a train up to Paris and registered at a small hotel.

It rained on the evening of the seventeenth and, without moon and stars, the city was as dark as it ever got, the blue-painted streetlamps casting no more than a dull glow on the empty streets. At eight-thirty, Adrian drove a panel truck to the entry of the Rue de la Huchette, and Ricard climbed in beside him. As the engine idled, Adrian handed Ricard a weapon, an M1935 7.65 semi-automatic pistol. "Know how to use it?" Adrian said.

"I think so. Is this the safety?"

"Yes, then pull the housing toward you to arm it. You've got eight rounds in there." Adrian drove to a street near the Impasse du Ruisseau and parked the truck. Ten minutes later, Henri and Jules appeared, and Adrian introduced them to Ricard; no last names, just Jules and Henri, rain dripping off the lowered brims of their hats. All four were tense, smoked cigarette after cigarette, and glanced too often at their watches. A few minutes before nine o'clock, Jules and Henri entered the empty **impasse** and found doorways on either side of the street. At the dead end of the street was the back of a factory, where, covered by a steel grille, some large, noisy machine was at work, drumming away and loud enough that they had to raise their voices almost to a shout in order to be heard.

Precisely at nine, Ricard, carrying a paper bag that held five thousand dollars, entered the **impasse** and waited at the far end of the street. Minutes passed. Nothing happened. Ricard looked back at Adrian, who stood to one side of the **impasse** entry, as though to say, **What do I do now?** Adrian made a calming gesture with his hand, **Wait.** Just as Ricard turned back to face the street, two shadows appeared, walking cautiously toward them. When Ricard could make out faces, he saw two men he'd never seen before.

One of the men gestured with a revolver, **Come toward us.**

Ricard approached, Vozki and Simon watched him carefully, especially watched his hands. Vozki said, voice raised above the drumming machine, "Do you have the money?"

Ricard handed over the paper bag. Vozki peered inside, and counted to himself. When he was done, Ricard said, "Where is Kasia?"

"You'll see her soon," Vozki said. "Now turn around and put your hands behind your back." Then Vozki circled behind him and tied his wrists with twine, tight enough to hurt. Then ran his hands over Ricard's raincoat and took the 7.65 pistol.

Vozki and Simon then walked Ricard back

toward the factory. When they were close to the end of the street, Ricard could make out a narrow alleyway that ran between the side of the factory and the next building, another factory. As he was led into the alley, he thought, **I'm finished. They're not coming.**

But they were. Jules and Henri had screwed long silencers into the barrels of their automatics, and the shots were like sibilant whispers. Vozki let go of Ricard and sank to his knees. "You'll never . . . ," he said as he died. Simon had been shot in the leg, and fallen facedown on the cobblestone, whining with pain. Jules turned him over, found Ricard's 7.65 automatic in his pocket, untied his hands, and gave it to him. "I believe this is yours," he said. Next he found Vozki's pistol beneath his chest, then took the clasp knife from his pocket. He opened it and said to Ricard, "Turn away."

Ricard heard Jules say, "Where's the girl?" Next he heard Simon scream, "The Hôtel Briand! The Hôtel Briand!"

"Where is it?"

"On the Rue du Rocher, by the Gare Saint-Lazare."

Jules said to Henri, "Go get the truck, we're taking the two of them with us. I'm leaving this one alive in case he's lying to us." Then he said to Simon, who was moaning and holding his leg, "You're not lying to us, are you?"

"No. That's the hotel. The girl is in room 502."

Panic at the edge of his voice, Simon whined, "I swear, monsieur, I swear it."

Jules then took Vozki's shirt in his hands and tore off a strip of fabric, then raised Simon's pant leg and tied the bandage around a bloody hole in his right leg. Adrian and Ricard loaded the wounded Simon and Vozki's body into the panel truck, then Jules slid into the driver's seat. "Where will you take them?" Ricard said.

"I'll leave them just outside a hospital. The doctors will take care of Simon's wound and they'll send the other one to the morgue. Maybe then they will call the police, or they won't, it doesn't matter."

Kasia remained a captive at the Hôtel Briand. At an apartment building across the street, Adrian and Ricard talked to the concierge, who let them into a vacant apartment on the third floor. From there, they watched the hotel. German officers were going in and out, some of them in SS uniforms. They would surely question Kasia, but they would get nothing out of her, at least not right away. "How to get her out of the building?" Ricard asked Adrian.

"Jules is still in Paris. I can call his hotel and ask him to help."

In midafternoon, Jules showed up at the apartment. "We need your help again," Ricard said. "They've got Kasia in their private hotel, there, across the street."

Jules watched for a time, then said, "Well, there

is a way, but it's going to make the Gestapo really mad."

"I don't care, do what you have to do," Ricard said.

They waited until late afternoon, a chilly, rainy November afternoon, then Jules left the apartment—they could see him from the apartment window—crossed the street, and disappeared into the alley that ran behind the back entrance to the hotel. Ten slow minutes passed, then Jules showed up, breathing hard and dusted with coal soot. "Now we wait," he said.

A minute or two later there was a muffled bang inside the hotel, a window shattered, and then, from the hotel's chimneys, a huge cloud of coal dust was blown over the street. It was still floating down when, in a window on the first floor of the hotel, an orange light flickered. German officers began to rush from the hotel, coughing in the sooty fog and, with bells ringing and siren wailing, a fire truck turned the corner and parked in front of the hotel. As the firemen unreeled their hoses, Kasia appeared. She'd been untied but was flanked by two Germans who held her arms. With a violent effort, she wriggled free, ran to one of the firemen, and cried out, "Save me!" As the firemen asked her what was going on, her two captors disappeared down the street.

Adrian, Jules, and Ricard had run down the stairs and out into the street, and when Kasia saw them, she ran to Ricard and embraced him. Then the three drove away in Adrian's panel truck, finally stopping by a small park. Kasia thanked the others, then Ricard offered her a cigarette, a Balto, from a packet with a cartoon of a sultan wearing a turban. Ricard lit the cigarette, Kasia inhaled and scowled. "A terrible cigarette! What became of your Gitanes?"

"The black-market supply dried up, so everyone smokes these."

"What happens now?" Ricard asked Adrian.

"Eventually, you and Kasia are going to have to disappear. For how long I can't say—maybe you can hide in Paris, maybe in France or America. Right now, you need to find a safe house, my friends. And don't tell anybody where it is."

Well, they **had** a safe house, rented at Adrian's direction, back in September—out in the Twelfth, a long way from nowhere by Parisian standards, overlooking the La Chapelle freight yards and the wine warehouses in Bercy. All it needed was furniture. Adrian drove the panel truck out to the flea market at the Porte de Vanves. On the way, Ricard asked about Jules: How did he come to know such clever tricks with explosives?

"Trained," Adrian said. "They train in Scotland, two months of it, learn every sort of mayhem and violence. I would say he is in France as an agent of the Special Operations people, though he would never admit that, but he's here to cause chaos, to blow things up, to cut telephone lines, to kill German officers."

At the market, they bought eight well-used mattresses, thin and lumpy with use but better than sleeping on the floor. They bought pots and pans and plates, including a heavy iron pot big enough to cook a stew for ten people, they bought mugs for coffee, and worn towels with faded blue stripes. "We must have a radio," Ricard said, found a table of radios, and turned them on and off until he found one, an old Philco in a walnut case with a curved top, that worked. They bought a small kerosene stove, then loaded everything into the panel truck and drove back toward central Paris on the Boulevard Brune.

And right into a French police roadblock.

Supervised by the wrong kind of **flic**. A stern fellow with gray hair and puppet lines by his mouth. He looked in the window of the panel truck, saw Adrian and Ricard and Kasia in the front seat, and smelled **artist, radical, communist, bohemian,** smelled the Saint-Germain-des-Prés on them. Oh, he knew who they were, alright, knew what they were, had never liked it in the past and didn't like it now. "Pull your truck over and start unloading," he said.

They did as they were ordered, leaving the mattresses inside. The household possessions didn't look their best in the gray drizzle. "What's all this?" he said, voice hard and unforgiving.

Kasia is so good, Ricard thought. She pretended to find the **flic** the sort of master she liked to obey, a disapproving and severe papa. She called him Monsieur l'Agent, starting each sentence with it. She was his to command.

"We are moving to a new apartment, Monsieur l'Agent."

"Where is that?"

"In the student district, sir, my friend and I will attend the Sorbonne in the fall."

What a clever little submissive you are, Kasia, your dominatrix, whoever she is lately, would be proud of your theatre. Ricard could see that all the cooing and Monsieur l'Agent–ing was having its effect. "A good thing, education, but you must study hard, **ma fille**"—**Jesus, my daughter, he calls her,** Ricard thought—"and not spend your time in idle frivolity."

"I promise to work so hard, sir," Kasia said.

Could that be, Ricard thought, the merest edge of a smile on that sourpuss of a face?

"Best to put your things back now," the **flic** said. "You don't want them to get wet in this rain."

The three hurriedly reloaded the panel truck and, just as Adrian shifted into first gear, the **flic** saluted them, touched the brim of his kepi with his index finger. "Now we go to work," Adrian said and headed for the safe house.

•

A day later, Ricard was again "Paul Ricard the novelist." Two weeks earlier, Julien Montrésor of Les Éditions Montrésor had scheduled a publication party for Ricard's new book, **Midnight in Trieste.** The party was held in the breakfast room of a hotel and, when Ricard arrived, promptly at seven, a waiter had already set out bottles of cheap, thin champagne, and was now wandering around the crowded room with a tray of canapés— quickly gobbled up by the hungry guests.

The party was much like those which had celebrated Ricard's previous publications, here and there he saw familiar faces—writers, editors, book reviewers—but most of the guests were invited from a list that Montrésor maintained, people who showed up, people who filled out the room. Ricard spoke briefly with Montrésor, who was complimentary but, stroking his Mephistophelian beard, kept looking over Ricard's shoulder to see who he should talk to next. Mixed in among the crowd were those people who could be useful to a publisher. Ricard didn't mind, Montrésor was who he was and climbed socially when he saw an opportunity, but he was a good publisher, he knew how to sell books, and royalty checks showed up in Ricard's mail.

Then, out of the crowd, an unexpected guest appeared: Colonel de Roux, who had apparently journeyed down from his house in Les Andelys for the party. Ricard was pleased that he'd come and said so.

"How goes the book?" de Roux said.

"It's gotten some good reviews, now we'll see if it sells."

"That's good to hear. By the way, I've brought a friend along, he's taken a room at the hotel and, when you have a minute, he'd like to congratulate you on your publication. He's in room 220, just above us."

A nameless friend, Ricard thought. **Which means I am going back to work.**

When the party ended, just about the time the last bottle of champagne had been drunk, Ricard went up to room 220 and tapped on the door. From inside, a deep, authoritative voice said, **"Entrez."**

Inside, two heavyset men in suits, one of them holding an automatic by his leg, and, seated in the shabby room's only chair, an aristocrat. He had the look, the look seen in portraits on the walls of fine houses, with a prominent nose and hair combed to one side, a member, Ricard thought, of the high elite of France, with a bearing that suggested power and prerogative. If he'd been seen getting out of a chauffeured car, the passerby would wonder, **Who** is **that?** Because he was clearly somebody important. He was, Ricard thought, no doubt titled, a **marquis** or a **comte,** owning estates and villages, and currently fighting for France, as his ancestors surely had. He did not offer a name and Ricard thought of him as "the officer."

"Good evening," the officer said. "I hope your party went well."

"It did, thank you."

"And the best of luck with your new book."

"Again, thank you." Ricard now sat on the edge of the bed in the darkened hotel room. Behind drawn curtains, rain was beating against the window.

Leaning forward, the officer said, "I've been talking to your controller." Which meant Adrian, though it took a moment for Ricard to make the connection. "And," the officer continued, "he tells me that you have established a safe house on the Rue Crémieux."

"We have. It is now furnished and ready for use."

The officer nodded, then said, "The war is changing, Monsieur Ricard. That won't be evident for a long time, but we must now think about the next stage, here in France. Not this year, maybe not even next year, but the time of invasion is approaching. British and American forces will attack the coast of France, somewhere in the north, and will begin to drive the German army back across the Rhine. This landing must be accompanied by an insurrection, thousands of Frenchmen and women will take part and their attacks—sabotage, train tracks ripped up, telegraph wires cut—will draw German troops away from coastal defense.

"But to do this, the people will need weapons:

rifles, Sten guns, heavy machine guns, and anti-tank weapons. These will be brought in by the British aircraft known as Westland Lysanders. These Lysanders, small, agile, and fast, are able to fly fifty feet above the ground and under enemy radar, they have been landing on French fields, bringing in weapons and munitions, and ferrying agents in and out of the country, since the early days of the occupation. Once the deliveries have been picked up, the arms will be stored in safe houses—private homes, factories, warehouses, and barns—and that will include the safe house on the Rue Crémieux. I know you understand all of this."

"Yes, I do," Ricard said. He had listened carefully to this officer, who was perhaps the most senior member of the Resistance he would ever meet.

"We are gathering **résistants** to work in this operation; reception committees for the Lysanders, people who know the countryside and can find open fields for landing zones, people who can store the weapons, people who can do the physical work of transporting them to safe houses. So, we want to recruit you, and whoever you can trust—family or lifelong friends—to work in this operation. It's dangerous work, the Gestapo knows this is coming and will try to disrupt the deliveries, will attempt to insert their own agents among the **résistants**, will send patrols to the countryside. So then, will you join us?"

"Tell me when and where," Ricard said. "And

I'll be there and bring at least one person along with me."

"Then we'll notify your controller, and he will provide the details."

The interview was over. As Ricard stood up to leave the room, the officer said, "And good luck to you, monsieur."

The coded telephone call came a week later, as the first flakes of December snow floated down on the Rue de la Huchette. Ricard had recruited Kasia to help in the operation and, following Adrian's direction, called her at nine in the evening, and she was at his apartment by nine-twenty. Adrian picked them up in his panel truck ten minutes later, then drove northwest from Paris, reaching the city of Beauvais an hour later. As they left the deserted streets of the city, Adrian gave each of them a flashlight, then handed Ricard a pencil-drawn map. Now Ricard lowered the window, despite the snow, in order to see better, and he searched for the road on the map. It didn't appear right away, and Ricard feared he'd missed it, but then, there it was. **Not much of a road,** Ricard thought, more like a cow path, with holes large enough to break an axle.

Adrian could drive no more than five miles an hour, foot riding the clutch pedal as the truck threatened to stall, then did stall, and Adrian had to use the ignition. Which worked, though twice

Ricard held his breath as the starter motor whined on and on and was close to killing the battery until, at last, it got the engine to turn over.

By ten-thirty they'd reached an old tire lying by the road, noted on the map next to an **X**. Adrian used his flashlight, which showed them a hedgerow border across the field. In fact, they discovered soon enough, wiping their shoes on the weeds, a cow pasture. As the three neared the hedgerow, the beam of a flashlight lit them up and a voice behind the light said, "Password."

"Avignon," Adrian replied.

The man in the darkness said, "Symphony," the countersign.

When they reached him they saw that he was not alone—five other men were ranged out behind him, some dressed in suits and overcoats, others wore workers' rough jackets and berets. All of them were armed, one with a shotgun, three with rifles, and the last, like the leader, had a Sten gun. "You have your truck?" the leader said.

"I do," Adrian said. "Will they fly in this weather?"

"It's clear in England, and they can land on snow—they can land on anything. The flight is due in a half hour. In the meantime, we have some shelter on the other side of the hedge." He led the three through an opening in the hedge, to a burned-out farmhouse. There they waited, smoking, and drinking sour wine from bottles without labels. **So,**

here is the French Resistance, Ricard thought. No names were given but, from conversation under a remaining part of the roof that gave them shelter, two of them were brothers, a third was a cousin, the other two longtime friends.

At twelve-thirty, they returned to the cow pasture. Then three of the men stood in a line which showed the direction of the wind—guiding the pilot to his landing path, and a fourth stood to one side. When they heard the engine of the approaching Lysander, the three turned on their flashlights, aimed at the Lysander, while the fourth signaled to the pilot with the Morse-code letter **C, dash-dot-dash-dot,** and the pilot responded with the airplane's landing lights, blinking the same letter.

The Lysander set its wheels down at the far end of the pasture and taxied up to the group. Then the pilot vaulted out, followed by another man, who said, "I'm called Foret. I'm the one you're waiting for, to take to Paris."

The pilot and three of the **résistants** then unloaded two aluminum cylinders from the Lysander and carried them, sometimes slipping on the snow, to Adrian's panel truck. Next they pushed the Lysander to a position facing the wind, the plane's pilot gave the Lysander full throttle, the wheels bounced across the uneven surface, then, almost at the end of the pasture, the plane lifted, just managing to clear the trees, and the sound of its engine faded away into the night. The **résistants** disappeared into the darkness, heading for the car they'd arrived in.

It was almost two in the morning before the panel truck reached the Rue Crémieux safe house where Adrian, Ricard, Kasia, and Foret carried the cylinders upstairs. They were breathing hard when they finished and Foret said, "Heavy, no? There are forty rifles for the Resistance in these things, and plenty of ammunition."

"When do we move them?" Adrian said.

"You don't, unless you think they would be safer somewhere else." In the light of the house they got a better look at Foret. He was dressed as a French businessman, in hat and overcoat, and carried a briefcase. He was, Ricard guessed, about forty years old. "So, back in France," Ricard said.

"Yes, at last. I used to be a salesman, of stationery, but I had problems with the Gestapo and fled to London, to de Gaulle."

"You met him?" Ricard said.

"Yes, for ten minutes. Otherwise I waited in a hotel. And waited."

"You wanted to come home to France," Adrian said.

"Yes, and to fight," Foret said.

By December of 1942, France was the land of the fugitive. Jews in hiding wanted to get to Spain and, eventually, to New York or Palestine. Agents of three countries, France, Poland, and Britain, were constantly on the move, working across borders in and out of the country. Then there were the people who could no longer bear living under occupation: Had the man at the next café table been a Gestapo agent? Or was he just nosy? He had surely tried to listen to the conversation. Also there were the usual fugitives, in flight from angry wives or mistresses, in flight from debt, in flight from the police for business crimes or prosecution for unpaid taxes. This was, taken altogether, a considerable number of people who wanted to be somewhere else.

So then, how to do that?

In a country where newspapers were edited by an occupying enemy, gossip became the only source for information. One forever heard a sentence begin: **My friend Louis says** . . . Or, **My doctor told me** . . . Or, **The woman who cleans my apartment has a friend who** . . . Yes, there was the BBC, but that was international news, rarely Parisian news, and one could be shot for listening to it. Fascist teenagers stood under apartment windows at nine in the evening, listening for the English voice, and ready to denounce the tenant.

In private, talking to friends and family, the possibility of getting out of the country was at least discussed. It was said that there were escape lines that ran all through France and down into Spain; were they just for secret agents? Or could civilians use them? **Do you know anybody?** became a common question. The answer was almost always no. Some of the fugitives kept to their apartments, others went about their daily business and pretended that nothing was wrong. The war wouldn't last forever, they would wait it out, and waiting, **attentisme,** became a kind of café philosophy.

Meanwhile, except for the storage of arms, the Rue Crémieux house stood empty but, for the civil servants in London, it was time to change that. They needed someplace safe for their agents moving through Paris and decided to use the Rue Crémieux house, which meant it had to be staffed with operatives. Three of them, as always: a radio operator, an agent, and a courier. As was customary for the Special Operations people, they sent their own, trained, radio operator to see Adrian. He was called Bondeau; a former bank clerk in Lyons, a tall, thin, gray man with a tall face, hair shaven high above his ears, and he was installed at the Rue Crémieux, running his radio aerial up the chimney. Ricard was chosen to be the resident agent, with Kasia working as courier.

SS Erhard Geisler sat in his office at the Hôtel Majestic and brooded about safe houses and escape lines. His SD superiors in Berlin were riding him hard about the subject. This form of resistance had to be stopped right away because it facilitated operations by the British enemy against the Reich. The agents who used these houses and traveled on the lines were often saboteurs. They blew up factories that produced war matériel and, fighting against the endless Russian forces, the Wehrmacht needed all the weapons and vehicles that could be produced—produced in the factories of occupied Europe.

How to operate against them? Geisler needed an agent, someone who could infiltrate the British scheme and identify the people who made it work. Only then, when they had names and addresses, could they make arrests. And the interrogations that would follow arrests would bring them more **résistants.** **That** would mean success. **That** would bring medals and promotion.

Now Ricard had to stay at the Rue Crémieux house, to take care of the agents who would be using it, and so, with a sigh in his heart, he abandoned his garret and installed himself in the safe house. The most difficult aspect to this move was that Ricard had to stay out of sight. He was used to his life in Paris, wandering the lovely old streets that always curved out of sight, stopping at his favorite haunts: this street market, that museum, the **quai** that ran along the edge of the Seine—his preferred place to stare at the river, along with a favored bridge or two—and the Saint-Germain-des-Prés cafés where he read novels instead of the dreadful newspapers.

Then, on a clear, starry night, Christmas close at hand, he had his first safe-house agent. After a coded telephone call from Adrian, the courier Kasia retrieved a British operative from the Gare du Nord, a young woman who used the alias **Beatrice.** Very good looking, Beatrice, an English girl who had grown up in the Valais, the French-speaking part of Switzerland. Kasia used the black-market shops and found her something to eat: a hard Cantal cheese, a decent baguette, a bowl of lentils, a bottle of Algerian wine, and one small, tired éclair. This last nearly brought Beatrice to tears, tough as she was, determined as she was. "Would you like to share?" she asked.

"No, my dear," Kasia said. "It's for you."

"I used to eat these, a treat, you know, sometimes after school. I fear I never really appreciated it, just something my **maman** had bought for me."

Beatrice couldn't say a word about where she'd been or where she was going or what she was tasked to do there. According to the talk in the cafés, the Gestapo was lately fierce, capturing and interrogating agents. The idea of Beatrice falling into their hands upset Ricard, perhaps because he was insufficiently coldhearted for the work he did now, but nonetheless he felt protective of this girl, though there wasn't much he could do to protect her. Some food, a night or two of safe sleep, then she would be on her way. Two days later, Kasia led her to a street in the Fourth Arrondissement and that was the last they saw of her.

•

The next agent was very different. Using the alias **Rafael**, he arrived, after a telephone call from Adrian, on Christmas Eve, and Kasia retrieved him from the Duroc Métro station. Rafael was a Spaniard, one of many who had managed to cross the Pyrenees into France after the defeat of the Spanish Republic's army in 1939. There were hundreds of such fugitives in France and, after 1940, most of them, intrepid fighters, joined the Resistance.

Rafael was then recruited by the SOE and assigned to stay in France and operate in the region north of Paris, Lower Normandy.

He was thirty or so, lithe and dark skinned, handsome, and shy. He sat in the kitchen of the Rue Crémieux house and ate sparingly. Surely he was famished, but, despite gentle urging from Ricard and Kasia, would eat no more than what he supposed to be his share, leaving food for other hungry people. "It is good of you," he said, in slow French, "to take me in and feed me."

"It is our pleasure to do this," Ricard said.

"And you fight alongside us in our war," Kasia added.

Rafael nodded slowly. "I know," he said. "But still, it is an old habit to leave something for those who will follow me, God willing."

Ricard poured the last of a bottle of the Algerian wine into a water glass and handed it to Rafael. "It is Christmas Eve, sir, and we must celebrate a little, as best we can." He then opened a new bottle and poured wine for himself and Kasia. "Joyeux Noël," he said.

Rafael then raised his glass and wished Ricard and Kasia a Joyeux Noël.

"Feliz Navidad," Ricard said. "Is that right?"

Rafael said, "Yes, Feliz Navidad. It makes me feel good just to say it. I spent last Christmas in a trench in Madrid, near the medical school. We shared an extra ration of bread that night, to celebrate."

"What did you do before the war?" Kasia asked.

"My family owned a wine bar, a **bodega**, in Madrid, and I worked there. I grew up in the bar, a lively place, people singing, lovers holding hands, dogs and cats and children all over the place. It was a fine way to grow up, hearing stories from travelers, listening to the conversations of students, who argued about our poets, which one was deep, which sentimental. They cared greatly about such things. Back then. In time, by 1936, I became a soldier, fighting the fascists. Still I fight them. But they don't go away."

"The day will come," Kasia said.

"To that," Rafael said, raising his glass. "Tell me, is it safe to go out at night?"

"No, it isn't," Ricard said. "The Gestapo is lately very active at night, before curfew."

"Curfew is at eleven?"

"Yes, but not tonight. The Germans have said

that tonight we are allowed to be out on the street until two."

"So people may attend midnight mass, Christmas mass," Rafael said.

"Yes, just so," Ricard said.

"That is what I would like to do, will it put you in danger? Probably I should go alone."

For a long moment, Ricard and Kasia looked at each other, then Ricard said, "No, we will go together."

"There is a church nearby?"

"There is a lovely church," Ricard said, "a few blocks from here. It is by a little park, where there's a tree with a plaque that says it is the oldest tree in Paris. Saint-Julien-le-Pauvre, the church is called."

Rafael brightened. "Then let's go there," he said. "Is it far?"

"No, we can walk there in twenty minutes," Ricard said.

They waited for a time, drinking the wine, then left the Rue Crémieux house and walked along the Seine. The Parisians were out in the streets—they had always liked the later hours of the evening— and a fine snow drifted down over the city on the windless night.

Three days later, Kasia picked up an agent who had been hiding in a cellar up in Saint-Denis. He carried with him a small leather bag which, when he set it down carefully on the floor of the kitchen, smelled like almonds.

"I've got explosives in here," he said, "808, it's called—**plastique,** to the French—so don't move it."

He was different than the first agents they'd hidden in the safe house, perhaps a soldier in the French army before the surrender, with a weathered, suntanned face and eyes aware of everything that went on around him. "Do you have anything to drink?" he asked Ricard, once he'd settled in.

"We have some wine," Ricard said. "Algerian wine."

"I'd like some of that. We drank it all the time when I was a legionnaire." He meant, Ricard knew, the French Foreign Legion. The soldier drank a lot of wine but was never close to getting drunk. He was in action, under orders, and, Ricard thought, would get no relief, from wine or anything else, until his mission was completed.

He stayed the night and left for the Gare de Lyon at dawn.

The tenth day of January, the holidays over. Now, to somehow live through the winter, which stretched out ahead forever. The low sky was oppressive, the color of ashes, as it would be for a long time, and there was frost on the windows of the houses and the shops.

Foret, the middle-aged stationery salesman who'd been brought in by Lysander, had been ordered to conduct surveillance on a large chemical factory in the town of Évreux, west of Paris, where several varieties of explosives were manufactured, a factory high on the list of facilities that the civil servants wanted destroyed.

Foret left his hiding place in Paris, where he'd gone after leaving the Rue Crémieux safe house, and rode the train to Évreux. There had been a military airfield here since the 1920s, and the chemical plant had been built, along with other industrial sites, to support the operations of French bombers and fighter planes. Now it was a German air base, which invited the attention of RAF planners.

The Romain et Fils Usine Chimique was situated at the western edge of the town, far from the Norman cathedral and the half-timbered houses and hotels of the **centre ville,** so Foret walked for a long time, shivering in the January chill, until he reached the neighborhood of the factory, where he found narrow streets of workers' housing and a few local bars and cafés. He found also Gestapo patrols, as well as local police on their bicycles—the factory and the airfield were crucial to the German war effort. Foret had a camera but was afraid to take it out of his briefcase. **Not here,** he thought.

He spent some time watching the factory, where the acrid smell of chemicals hung in the still air and made it hard to breathe. The lights were on in the windows, and vans at the loading dock behind the three-story building were being filled with metal drums. A busy place, with three eight-hour shifts, he'd been told. Nearby was a bar where he could contact the local Resistance group, which had been ordered to attack the plant: eliminate the guards posted by the doors, then set the factory ablaze. Once the flames reached the vats of chemicals, there would be explosions and fires. Most of the plant's workers were not expected to survive.

Foret entered the bar and asked for Claude, his Resistance contact, then took a coffee to one of the empty tables. Claude turned out to be a stout young man who wore a leather apron over his worker's outfit. Foret gave the **parole** and Claude responded. "We've been expecting a Resistance agent," he said. "What do you need from us?"

"I'm here to organize the destruction of the chemical works," Foret said.

Claude nodded. "Yes, it's an obvious target. The British tried to bomb it last month, but it's hard to see from the air, the German fighter planes took off immediately, from the local airfield, and the bombers turned around and beat it back to England."

Foret was sympathetic. "I know. This job has to be done on the ground."

"You can try, but the factory is carefully guarded," Claude said.

"Surely your friends can deal with that."

"Yes, I suppose they could, but they're not in a hurry to start trouble."

"No?"

"No. You must have seen the workers' housing on your way here, there are five hundred jobs at this plant. Good jobs, well-paid jobs. When the plant goes, all those jobs go with it. Which means we will all wind up as slave laborers in German factories."

"I'll tell them that," Foret said. "The people who want the plant destroyed, that they'll have to think of something else."

But Foret was lying and Claude knew it. "Yes, that's what you should do," he said.

This is how it is when you're at war. Foret didn't say that, but both men knew it was true—that the people who had issued the order were not going to **argue,** they were not going to **negotiate,** they had ordered their agents to destroy a certain target, so it would be destroyed.

"I will be in contact with you," Foret said.

"Then **au revoir,**" Claude said, left the table, and headed for the door.

Foret almost called out to him—perhaps they should talk this over for a little while longer. But then, with a shrug, he left the bar and began to walk back toward the Évreux railroad station. He almost made it, but Claude had reacted quickly to the threat and defended himself, and the chemical plant workers, without hesitation—Foret was a secret operative, who knew where he might be hiding. So Claude had made the telephone call to the Gestapo.

A few hundred feet from the railway station,

a Gestapo Citroën pulled up next to Foret, who briefly tried to run for it, but the Gestapo operatives jumped out of their car, knocked Foret to the ground, hauled him to his feet, then threw him in the back of the car. Ten minutes later he was hustled into the Gestapo's Évreux headquarters, taken to the cellar, and tied to a chair. They let him sit there and think about it for an hour, then an officer, whom the sergeant addressed as Sturmbannführer—Major— Geisler, sat in a chair and lit a cigarette while the sergeant took off his tunic, rolled up his sleeves, produced a rubber truncheon, and tapped Foret on the knee.

Pain exploded in Foret's kneecap. He couldn't believe how much it hurt, the man had simply snapped the instrument with his wrist. "We're just getting warmed up," Geisler said. "This should take a half hour, more or less."

"What do you want to know?" Foret said, panic in his voice.

The sergeant tapped him again and Geisler said, "Can you repeat that? I didn't quite hear you."

"Just ask, I'll tell you anything." Now he was pleading.

"We've heard there is a safe house, somewhere in the Twelfth, where is it?"

"On the Rue Crémieux."

"What number?"

"I don't think it has a number."

Tap.

This one was a little harder, the sergeant was a master of his craft, and Foret heard himself say **ah**, not loud, the syllable forced from him.

"Soon you'll sing like a nightingale," Geisler said, and nodded to the sergeant.

Foret cried out, "No more!"

Geisler stood up, then knelt in front of Foret, tied tight to the chair. "Now I shall tell you what we're going to do," he said, the menace in his voice deeper as he pitched it to a level of quiet gentility. "We're going to keep you here, and we're going to have a look at the Rue Crémieux. Next you will accompany us, and you will indicate which house the British agents are using. If you fool us . . ."

"Yes, I understand," Foret said.

Geisler was reflective as he said, "Perhaps you do, we shall see."

Ricard and Kasia continued to work at the safe house, every two or three days another agent appeared, then vanished the following day, usually at night. Kasia brought in what food she could find, Ricard stayed hidden. Then, on the seventeenth of January, late on a gray afternoon, Kasia said, "They're in the neighborhood, Germans in civilian suits, expensive suits."

Ricard went out to see for himself. Kasia was right, the Gestapo was working the local streets. They were trying to be subtle, reading newspapers in the cafés, strolling down the street, insouciant as could be, but, from their dress, from their military posture, from their proper haircuts, it was clear as day who they were, what they were. They had a bad effect on Ricard, he was afraid of them, and he suspected they were there for him. So he took a chance, went to the Rue de la Huchette, and took the 7.65 automatic from the drawer of his desk, just beneath his typewriter and the manuscript of his new book. He was not going to be taken alive and tortured by the Gestapo and, if they tried to arrest him, he was going to fight. That would be the end, but he meant to take two or three of them with him.

By nightfall, an ice fog gathered over the city, then wind-driven snow began to cover the street. From the window of the safe house, Ricard could only just see the La Chapelle railway tracks; snow was swirling above them, driven by the wind that sighed at the corners of the building. On the tracks, a lone switching engine made slow way into the tunnel.

On the Rue Crémieux, a black Mercedes cruised past the house, the yellow beams of its headlights cutting through the darkness. As Ricard and Kasia watched, the car stopped, then backed up, and, when a door opened, the domelight revealed two Gestapo officers in front and two men in overcoats in back. When the two men in the back left the car, Ricard saw Foret and a pear-shaped man, holding on to his hat in the wind. Foret pointed at the house, the pear-shaped man nodded, then both returned to the Mercedes.

"We're fucked, Kasia," Ricard said.

"I saw them."

"So, it's time to leave," Ricard said. The radio operator Bondeau shut down his transmission, closed the lid on the W/T radio, which made it look like a typewriter case, and headed for the door. "Good luck," Bondeau said. "See you again someday."

"I have to give the alert," Ricard said.

He called Adrian's number and, through the storm's static on the line, Adrian said, "Yes?"

"Solitaire," Ricard said. The word was a warning signal, it meant **Drop whatever you're doing and run like hell.**

"What's happened?" Adrian said.

"I just saw Foret and what I think was a Gestapo officer in a suit. Foret had guided him to the house."

"Foret," Adrian mused, then said, "You'll have to take care of him."

"Take care of him?"

"You know what I mean, he's put the entire operation in danger, so you'll have to . . . do what needs to be done."

"And then?"

"Get on a train, go somewhere."

"Alright."

"Let me know when it's finished," Adrian said, and hung up.

"We have to find Foret," Ricard said. "He has to be eliminated." He put on his hat and scarf and raised the collar of his overcoat. Kasia was waiting for him at the door, her worker's cap tilted down on her forehead.

"Anything you want in here?" Ricard said.

"No. Why?"

"You won't see it again."

From the telephone, a double-whirring ring. Ricard picked up the receiver before it rang again. It was Leila. "I just spoke to Adrian, he said you have a job to do and then you'll have to leave Paris. Where can we meet?"

"The Gare de Lyon is close, we'll meet there."

"Will you wait for me?"

"Yes."

Ricard and Kasia left the house and went out into the storm. Up the street, Ricard could see the light beams coming toward him as the Mercedes backed up. Ricard took the 7.65 from his coat pocket, made sure the clip was full, then snapped the magazine back in place and armed the weapon.

Ricard took careful steps through the dry snow, crossed the street, and waited. Very slowly, the

Mercedes approached him, and it was still moving when he stepped off the sidewalk and fired through the driver's window. From the other side of the car, he could barely hear the reports of Kasia's little .25, but the passenger slumped over, his head in the driver's lap, as the driver died with his forehead resting on the steering wheel. From the backseat, SS Erhard Geisler stumbled out of the car with his hands in the air. "Don't shoot," he said, raising his voice above the wind. A ruse. He didn't intend to surrender, and when his hand reached inside his coat, Kasia shot him below the left eye. "Don't," he said, and Kasia shot him again. He sat down on the snow, touched the wound with his finger, then fell backward and lay still.

Ricard swung the 7.65 toward Foret, who raised his hands, his eyes wide with fear. Then Ricard did what had to be done and fired twice through the window, the bullets punching holes circled by crushed glass. Foret disappeared. Ricard tore the door open. Foret lay still, sprawled on the car's floor, his head having landed on the running board when Ricard opened the door. To make sure, Ricard fired once more, hitting Foret in the temple, the wound bleeding red onto the snow.

Kasia and Ricard got away from the car as fast as they could, then, out of breath, they found an apartment house with an open door and took refuge in the vestibule. "Now we're in for it," Ricard said. "You don't kill Gestapo officers, they'll be all over the place in minutes."

"The storm will slow them down," Kasia said.

"Not much. Their big Citroëns have front-wheel drive. We'll have to hide, and not in our apartments."

"There's a place we can go," Kasia said. "Do you remember we once met in a club, on the Rue de Provence, out in the Ninth? Le Coup de Foudre, it's called. My friends there will take care of us."

"I do remember," Ricard said. "Women in black, smoking with cigarette holders. But I can't go there yet, so I'll contact you later."

"Be careful, Ricard," Kasia said.

Ricard took her by the shoulders and kissed her on the forehead. Then Kasia headed for the nearest Métro.

It was unwise to run down a street in an occupied city, so Ricard hurried as fast as he dared. When he reached the garret on the Rue de la Huchette, he had to sit down for a time, his hands shaking, his heart beating too hard. But he couldn't linger, he had to leave Paris. He opened his canvas valise, found a shirt, a pair of trousers, change of underwear, toothbrush, and razor, and laid all of it in the valise. Then he hesitated: Am I coming back here? Or will I never see it again? He didn't know, but he had no time to worry about it.

He glanced at his watch, then put the manuscript

of **The Investigator**, bound with rubber bands, into the valise and set the 7.65 on top of it. When he'd closed the valise, the image of the gun and the novel stayed with him. A good subject for a painted still life, he thought. **Paris, 1943.**

Leila would be waiting for him, he knew, so he walked quickly to the Gare de Lyon. The waiting room was packed, a sea of faces: some travelers, some fugitives from the storm, some fugitives. Then he saw Leila, and their embrace was intense; he held her against him as tightly as he could. "I was afraid you wouldn't come," she said, voice unsteady.

"There was no chance of that," Ricard said, smoothing back her hair. "We need a safe place to meet. There's a student hotel on the street that runs up to the Panthéon. I have things to do, so I'll meet you there tonight."

"Be careful, love," Leila said.

Ricard kissed her on the forehead and went out into the storm.

ESCAPE

NOW RICARD HAD NOWHERE TO GO. THE SAFE house on the Rue Crémieux was no longer safe, and a Gestapo Citroën was parked on the Place Saint-Michel, just beyond the Rue de la Huchette. So, valise in hand, he headed over to Éditions Montrésor on the Rue Jacob. The receptionist opened the inner office door, Montrésor saw who was coming to see him and said, "Ricard, come into the office," then quickly shut the door behind him. "They're looking for you, Ricard, what did you **do**?"

"A fight with a Gestapo officer, for him it ended badly."

Montrésor nodded, not sorry to hear bad news

for the Gestapo, but his face was tense with anxiety. "They've been here twice, they've been to my house in Neuilly, you are a much-wanted man."

"I need somewhere to hide."

"Not in Paris. Not in **France.** You have to get out of the country."

Ricard took a deep breath, Montrésor was right and Ricard knew it.

"The word is around that you're an English spy," Montrésor said.

"Well, I've . . . done things. For the Resistance."

"Then they'll have to hide you. Because when the Gestapo finds out that someone hid you, that's the end of him **and** his family. The Germans are worse every day, their appetite for cruelty . . ."

"So, I shouldn't be here."

"I'm sorry, Ricard, I'd like to help you, but . . ."

"Yes, I understand."

"This building has a back door that leads to an alley, you should use it." Montrésor was silent, anxious for Ricard to leave.

"Thank you, I'll take the back door."

"Contact me when you're safe," Montrésor said.

"I will," Ricard said, and left the office.

Finally, he decided he had to use the hotel where he had arranged to meet Leila, so climbed the hill to the Sainte-Geneviève church and the Panthéon and approached the reception desk.

At the desk, he paid in advance for two nights. "Your passport, monsieur" . . . the clerk ran his

finger over the signature in the guest register . . .
"Ricard." As Ricard handed over his passport,
the clerk said, "Don't worry yourself, monsieur. The
police pick them up every night and return them
in the morning."

"Yes. I know," Ricard said.

The clerk gave him a big iron key on a wooden
plaque that said CHAMBRE 18.

Ricard climbed the stairs, looked around the
room, then, valise in hand, went back downstairs
and headed for the post office where they asked to
see his passport before he entered the telephone
booth, so he went off to find a café with a telephone.
As usual, Leila's contact number was answered by a
woman's voice, and Ricard gave her the name of his
hotel. Then he called a friend, another writer, who
said, "Don't call here again, Ricard," and hung up.
The Gestapo's dossier, Ricard thought, had better
information than he'd realized. He tried another
friend, a friend from his time at the Sorbonne,
whose wife answered and said, "I'll tell him you
called. He'll surely call you back," but she did not
ask for a telephone number.

Desperate, Ricard went back to the hotel where,
at the reception desk, the clerk was speaking on the
telephone, his voice low and confidential. When
he'd hung up, Ricard said, "I'm leaving the hotel,
give me back my passport."

"Oh, monsieur, I regret . . ."

Ricard unbuckled his valise and put the muzzle

of the 7.65 under the clerk's chin, forcing his head back. "Give it to me, you sneaky little bastard, or I'll blow the top of your head off."

The clerk, with trembling hands, returned his passport. "We'll see you after the war," Ricard said, and walked quickly out the door.

Now he couldn't wait for Leila at the hotel, but he could, he thought, intercept her when she arrived. There was a small park across the street, and, as the snow drifted down, Ricard sat on a bench that faced the doorway of the hotel. It was after five, a night as black as any Ricard remembered, but he could see the hotel well enough. **Where is she,** he thought. As he waited, the cold began to work its way through his overcoat and he pulled it tighter. People sometimes died of the cold in Paris when they had nowhere to shelter—the newspapers noted the death with one paragraph: Monsieur X, sometimes Madame X, was found frozen to death in an alley, in a doorway, sitting on a bench in the park. A still figure, Ricard thought, face glazed with ice.

An hour passed and it was getting colder as the evening wore on. If he went to a café, he might miss Leila, and she was now his only hope to get out of Paris, to get out of France. The Gestapo was watching the railway stations but, he thought, Leila would know a way around that. Again he looked at his watch, five hours until curfew, but curfew didn't matter when it came to an operative like Leila.

Ricard clapped his hands together in order to warm them, the cold had seeped through his gloves, and his fingers were stiff and numb. How much longer could he last? He rose from the bench and walked around the perimeter of the park. And realized that his feet were damp—the melting snow was soaking its way through his shoes. All he could do now was find a café with a telephone and try Leila's number again.

Halfway down the hill, a student café, crowded on a cold night because, when there wasn't enough heat in an apartment, a café with a wood or kerosene stove was a refuge. Ricard sat at the bar—all the tables were taken—and ordered a brandy. The barman stared at him, poured out his brandy, and slid it across the zinc bar. Then, without speaking, he handed Ricard a sheet of paper. A Gestapo circular with a faded photograph at the top, a mimeographed photograph of poor quality, but it was him. In the text below, a reward of ten thousand francs was offered for information leading to the arrest of Paul Ricard, of 9, Rue de la Huchette. Ricard handed the circular back to the barman, who said, "Drink your brandy, monsieur, one needs something on a night like this, but then you'll have to go."

"I understand," Ricard said, slugged down his brandy, went back out into the night, and returned to the park across from the hotel. A few minutes later, a black Citroën pulled up to the door of the hotel and two men in suits entered. Gestapo. That bastard of a reception clerk had called the police, Ricard thought, he had been denounced. Nothing new in Paris, but now it was his turn. And he could only hope that Leila hadn't visited the hotel in his absence. What if she had? What if she'd asked for him at the reception desk? What if the Gestapo was there for **her**?

Sick at heart, he waited. Five minutes went by, then ten. At last, the two Gestapo men left the hotel and returned to their car. Ricard squatted down behind a bench as the Citroën's lights illuminated the park. Then the lights disappeared as the car turned onto another street. **Just the two of them,** he thought. No Leila.

Again, he began to walk. The fierce cold burning the skin of his face, the powdery snow sometimes lifted by the wind and sent dancing in the air. **So then,** he thought, if Leila was not coming to his rescue, that left Adrian, his last chance. What had Adrian said, in their last conversation?

"Get on a train, go somewhere." What if Adrian had done that very thing, in response to the **Solitaire** warning?

Ricard returned to the student café, where the barman was not happy to see him. So Ricard was contrite, apologetic—eating crow was, after all, preferable to freezing to death. "Forgive me, monsieur, it's the occupation, it's made me forget my manners."

"You'll get into trouble if you go on that way," the barman said.

"Yes, you are right. I apologize." Ricard extended his hand and, after a beat, the barman took it in his own. "I would be very grateful if you would permit me to use the telephone."

"Very well," the barman said, not entirely appeased.

Ricard lifted the receiver and dialed Leila's number, but there was no answer. Then he tried Adrian. The telephone rang and rang, nobody answered. **I dialed the wrong number,** Ricard thought, and tried again, with the same result. He looked at his watch, it was now nine twenty-five, the eleven o'clock curfew was approaching and that would mean real trouble.

Ricard looked around the café and saw a girl, likely a student, sitting alone at a table. Ricard ordered a coffee, took it over to the girl's table, and said, "Do you mind if I join you? It's crowded in here tonight."

The girl considered it, then said, "**Avec plaisir,** monsieur." She didn't mean the words, **with pleasure;** her response was a formula. Still, he sat down, took off his wet gloves, and wrapped his ice-cold hands around the warm cup.

Ricard saw that the girl had nearly finished her glass of red wine and said, "Mademoiselle, would you permit me to buy you another wine?"

The girl looked at her watch and scowled. "I must go back to my room, but . . . if you want to, I would appreciate it."

Ricard went to the bar and brought back two

glasses of wine. "What brings you out in the storm?" Ricard said.

The girl shrugged. "I couldn't bear to stay in that little room any longer, so I called a friend, but he hasn't shown up."

"Your boyfriend?"

"Oh, of a sort. What brings you out tonight, monsieur . . . ?"

"Ricard. Paul Ricard."

"I'm called Sabine."

"What brings me out in the storm, Sabine, is that I'm locked out of my apartment, so I'm trying to figure out where to go. All the hotels are full."

"You really have nowhere to stay?" Again, she looked at her watch. "Curfew will be in a little while, you'll have to go somewhere."

Ricard shrugged and smiled. She was a pretty girl, he thought, with thick, black hair and full lips—not pink, almost red, even though she wore no lipstick.

"Well," Sabine said, "I have a room, not much, a student room, but you can stay there tonight."

"That would be very kind of you," Ricard said, gratitude warming his heart.

Sabine laughed. "Wait till you see the room, maybe you won't be so grateful." Preparing to go out into the storm, she drew a red wool muffler around her face, just below her eyes, and pulled her hat, a roomy version of a beret, down to her eyebrows. "Now I'm ready," she said.

As Ricard prepared to go, he said, "It might not be a good idea to have me in your room. The Gestapo is after me, so you could get into real trouble."

"Let's go," she said. "I can't worry about the Boche, because that's what they want me to do." As they approached the door, Sabine said, "What did you do to get the Boche after you?"

"Better if I don't tell you, but they would really like to arrest me."

Out on the street, the two bent against the wind, walking carefully in the snow. "I'm already cold," Sabine said. "Put your arm around my shoulders." As Ricard held her, she drew him against her by circling her arm around his waist. "There," she said. "Now we look like a couple. A nice student couple. What is it you do, Paul?"

"I write books."

"I don't think I've read them," she said. "In my literature class, we only go to the nineteenth century: Stendhal, the poet Gautier. Are you famous?"

"Well known, for what I do, I'm a genre novelist. I write about detectives and spies."

Sabine turned them right on the Rue Saint-Jacques. "Not far now," she said.

From some distance, Ricard heard the rumble of a powerful engine. Sabine stopped and said, "What's that?"

"A Citroën Traction Avant. The SS favorite."

Ricard knew that the officers in the Gestapo car

were looking for him. He could hear the car stop, then the slam of a door and, after half a minute, the door slammed again, and the Citroën moved down the street. It was difficult for Ricard to hear over the sound of the wind, and standing still, trying to pick up direction, was the only way to do it. First, the sound moved closer, and Sabine put a hand on his arm, then the car stopped again, an officer searching the shadowed doorways, he thought—then it moved away.

Suddenly, a blast of sound rose above the wind, a loud-hailer, a bullhorn. The voice had the metallic ring of speech amplified by a microphone:

"Ricard, we know you're out here. Give yourself up and it will go easier for you."

"Let's try for your room," Ricard whispered.

They set off up the Rue Saint-Jacques, past shuttered stores and restaurants—the owners had, because of the storm, gone home. Ricard and Sabine tried to walk quickly over the frozen snow. Then, a single word from the loud-hailer: "Halt!"

The Citroën was, Ricard guessed, maybe a block away, but they had been seen. Ricard knelt down and started to open his valise, meaning to get hold of the 7.65 automatic and try to chase the Citroën away. Then shots rang out, four or five, and, instinctively, Ricard stood and started to run, Sabine at his side. A few seconds later, Ricard slipped and fell facedown on the snow. "Are you wounded?" Sabine said.

"No," Ricard said, "I fell."

Then Sabine sank down to her knees. "I am shot," she said. "Merde, it hurts. Help me, Paul."

Desperately, Ricard looked around him and saw a small park, the Jardins de Navarre, it was called. In the spring, he'd sat on a bench there and read a book. Now he said, "Can you walk?"

"Yes. I have to."

Ricard helped her to her feet and they ran toward the park. This didn't take much time, just enough for another **Halt!** from the Gestapo officer.

As they entered the park, Ricard looked desperately for a place to hide.

A moment later he saw the fountain—turned off for the winter. But fountains, he knew, had an operating apparatus hidden beneath them. "Over there," Ricard said, but, as he started to move, Sabine again sank to her knees.

"Save yourself, Paul," she said.

"No," Ricard said, and hauled Sabine to her feet as she gasped from the pain. As they reached the fountain, there were more shots fired from the Citroën, but Ricard barely noticed. Beneath the fountain, an old wooden door. Ricard pushed against it, but it was locked. Then he stood on one leg and smashed his heel against the door, in the place where he calculated the lock would be, and the door opened.

The Gestapo looked for them in the park. Through cracks at the edge of the door, Ricard could see flashlight beams, hunting this way and that, and at one point, a Gestapo officer stood somewhere nearby and said, in German-accented French, his voice loud, "Well, I guess they're not here." Then, a few minutes later, with the icy cold and the wind, they'd had enough of searching and went off to find different victims.

Ricard and Sabine made it back to Sabine's room on the Rue Saint-Jacques, where Sabine took her shirt off and Ricard got a look at the bullet wound, in Sabine's back, just below her shoulder blade. It had bled very little, and they both thought this had something to do with the cold. "Do you have a telephone?" Ricard said.

"On a little table, at the foot of the stairs."

Ricard called Leila's number, left a message, and Leila immediately called back. "I'm with a friend who has a bullet wound and we need a doctor."

"It's after curfew," Leila said. "Can it wait?"

"I don't think so."

"Give me the address and wait in the vestibule, a panel truck will pick you up and take you to a doctor."

"A panel truck? After curfew?"

"He has papers that say he delivers medical supplies, he can go anywhere at any time."

The doctor's office was in the Avenue Montaigne, which meant a wealthy, upper-class clientele. Ricard rang the bell, and the doctor himself let them in, the concierge gone for the night. The doctor had white hair, was maybe sixty, and was wearing a plaid bathrobe and pajamas. "Come in," he said. "Your friend is waiting for you."

As the doctor took Sabine into his examining room, Ricard and Leila sat on a couch in the office reception.

"Will your friend be alright?" Leila said.

"I think so. I had a look at the wound, the bullet hit at an angle, maybe came out somewhere in her armpit, though I didn't see anything there. She's lucky; if the bullet had entered in a straight line it would have gone through her heart."

"How do you come to know her?"

"I don't. I couldn't go home, I still can't, can't go anywhere without being caught, there are circulars posted all over Paris. Anyhow, I was in a café near the Mont Sainte-Geneviève and she said I could stay in her room. On the way there, the Boche caught up to us and fired a few shots—I doubt they know they hit anything."

"The Gestapo guards every hospital and clinic in Paris, looking for gunshot wounds."

"I know. Thank heaven for the doctor," Ricard said.

"Yes, he's a well-known internist but, at night, he's a Resistance doctor."

Leila paused a moment, then said, "I have news to relay to you, Ricard, important news, from the people in London, the civil servants who run at least some of the networks, the escape lines, the safe houses, all of it. They have asked me to tell you that, for the moment, at least, your days of fighting the occupation are over. You're now like some kind of poisonous plant, it's not safe to be anywhere near you, so it's time to go, to leave France. You can refuse, of course, they will accept your answer politely, but, if it's the wrong answer, if it's **No, I won't,** you'll be dead in an hour. That's how it has to be done, **chéri,** I'm sure you understand."

Ricard thought it over, what it would mean to him, and then said, "If I have to run, Leila, will you run with me?"

"I will. I'm in love with you, Ricard, I won't let you go."

"And Kasia?"

"She must also leave, she's being told as we sit here."

"Alright, Leila, we'll run. Where will we be safe?"

"Spain, at first, then, in time, Istanbul. My family will take care of us, and Turkey is a neutral state, so you'll be safe there."

"And when do we leave?"

"Tomorrow. The doctor will let us stay here overnight."

Kasia traveled west, crossing the frontier into Switzerland, in time reaching a chalet, deep in the mountains, where a very rich woman friend meant to wait out the war. Kasia was greeted warmly, by good friends from Paris, and given a glass of well-aged Burgundy. "Will you go back to Paris?" her friend asked.

"Maybe someday," Kasia said. "For now, I am very tired; is there somewhere I can rest?"

"Your bedroom is upstairs," her friend said. "Come, I'll show you where, and I have a night-gown you can wear."

Leila and Ricard fled south, on the old roads, from village to village, from Combres to Retournac to Saint-Hostien. Somewhere beyond the Loire the snow had gone, revealing winter fields. Sometimes they took local trains, three-car trains that rattled along at twenty miles an hour and stopped at tiny stations. Once they took an old bus that belched blue smoke from its exhaust pipe. Sometimes they rode in farmers' wagons pulled by old horses, some-times they walked. Sometimes they saw church steeples in the distance, which meant villages with little hotels. The skies were blue in the south, where a weak sun suggested that spring might come, someday in the months ahead. In time they reached a village on the coast, and there found a grizzled old rogue with a milky eye who took them, by felucca, to a village in Spain. The village had an eight-room hotel, and they stayed there for a few days. As they lay in bed one morning, a breeze ruffling the sheer curtains by an open window, they talked about the future, about the end of the war, about, someday, going back to Paris.

ABOUT THE AUTHOR

ALAN FURST, widely recognized as the master of the historical spy novel, is the author of **Midnight in Europe, Mission to Paris,** and many other bestsellers. Born in New York, he lived for many years in Paris, and now lives on Long Island.

alanfurst.net
Facebook.com/AlanFurstBooks